"Let Go Of Me!" Genevieve Screamed. "Let Go Of Me This Instant Or You'll— You'll Be Sorry!"

She was threatening him? Unbelievable. The woman clearly had more nerve than sense. Twisted together on the cold, snowy ground, Taggert locked his legs around hers and tightened the grip he had on her waist. "Pay attention, lady. I'm in charge now. You do what I tell you. Understand?"

A whimper escaped her throat. "Yes," she gasped.

"Now get up."

She stayed where she was.

He took a threatening step forward. "Now."

She flinched and threw up her hands. "Okay, okay!"

He reached down to help her up, and the moment he did, she threw her weight backward, yanking him forward. Off balance, he stumbled. It was all the advantage his adversary needed. She rolled away, sprang to her feet and bolted.

"Lady, you don't know who you're dealing with!" She had no idea at all.

Dear Reader,

It's February and that means Cupid is ready to shoot his arrow into the hearts of the six couples in this month's Silhouette Desire novels. The first to get struck by love is Teagan Elliott, hero of Brenda Jackson's *Taking Care of Business*, book two of THE ELLIOTTS continuity. Teagan doesn't have romance on his mind when he meets a knock-out social worker…but when the sparks fly between them there's soon little else he can think of.

In *Tempt Me* by Caroline Cross, Cupid doesn't so much as shoot an arrow as tie this hero up in chains. How he got into this predicament…and how he gets himself out is a story not to be missed in this second MEN OF STEELE title. Revenge, not romance, plays a major role in our next two offerings. Kathie DeNosky's THE ILLEGITIMATE HEIRS trilogy continues with a hero hell-bent on making his position as his old flame's new boss a *Reunion of Revenge*. And in *His Wedding-Night Wager* by Katherine Garbera, the first of a new trilogy called WHAT HAPPENS IN VEGAS…, a jilted groom gets the chance to make his runaway bride pay.

Seven years is a long time for Cupid to do his job, but it looks like he might have finally struck a chord with the stranded couple forced to reexamine their past relationship, in Heidi Betts's *Seven-Year Seduction*. And rounding out the month is a special Valentine's Day delivery by author Emily McKay, who makes her Silhouette Desire debut with *Surrogate and Wife*.

Here's hoping romance strikes you this month as you devour these Silhouette Desire books as fast as a box of chocolate hearts!

Best,

Melissa Jeglinski

Melissa Jeglinski
Senior Editor
Silhouette Desire

Please address questions and book requests to:
Silhouette Reader Service
U.S.: 3010 Walden Ave., P.O. Box 1325, Buffalo, NY 14269
Canadian: P.O. Box 609, Fort Erie, Ont. L2A 5X3

CAROLINE CROSS

Tempt Me

Silhouette® Desire

Published by Silhouette Books

America's Publisher of Contemporary Romance

SILHOUETTE BOOKS

ISBN 0-373-76706-4

TEMPT ME

Visit Silhouette Books at www.eHarlequin.com

Printed in U.S.A.

Books by Caroline Cross

Silhouette Desire

Dangerous #810
Rafferty's Angel #851
Truth or Dare #910
Operation Mommy #939
Gavin's Child #1013
The Baby Blizzard #1079
The Notorious Groom #1143
The Paternity Factor #1173
Cinderella's Tycoon #1238
The Rancher and the Nanny #1298
Husband—or Enemy? #1330
The Sheikh Takes a Bride #1424
Sleeping Beauty's Billionaire #1489
Trust Me #1694
Tempt Me #1706

*Men of Steele

CAROLINE CROSS

always loved to read, but it wasn't until she discovered romance that she felt compelled to write, fascinated by the chance to explore the positive power of love in people's lives. She grew up in Yakima, Washington, the "Apple Capital of the World," attended the University of Puget Sound and now lives outside Seattle, where she (tries to) work at home despite the chaos created by two telephone-addicted teenage daughters and a husband with a fondness for home-improvement projects. Pleased to have recently been #1 on a national bestseller list, she was thrilled to win the 1999 Romance Writers of America RITA® Award for Best Short Contemporary Novel and to have been called "one of the best" writers of romance today by *Romantic Times BOOKclub*. Caroline believes in writing from the heart—and having a good brainstorming partner. She loves hearing from readers and can be reached at P.O. Box 47375, Seattle, Washington 98146. Please include a SASE for reply.

One

John Taggart Steele stood motionless in the shifting shadows that edged the towering stand of evergreens.

Snowflakes swirled in the icy air around him, swept from the treetops high overhead by a capricious wind. Narrowing his eyes against the October sun, he raised his binoculars to zero in on the tidy A-frame cabin in the clearing five hundred yards away, only to jerk the glasses away as his cell phone vibrated. Ripping it from the clip on his belt, he glanced at the screen and saw the call was from Steele Security's Denver office. He hit the receive button and slapped the instrument to his ear. "What?"

"Looks like it's her, all right." As calm as a summer day, his brother Gabe's voice held neither reproach at the brusque greeting nor satisfaction as he delivered the long-awaited confirmation.

Taggart said nothing, merely waited.

"The truck was recently registered to a woman calling herself Susan Moore. The previous owner is a Laramie grad student who says he sold the vehicle three weeks ago to a cocktail waitress at the bar he frequents. He described Bowen to a T, said she was 'a real sweet little thing.' She paid cash for the vehicle and confided she was headed south to see her ailing grandpa."

"Laramie, huh?"

Gabe seemed to know exactly what Taggart was thinking. "Yeah. When she left Flagstaff, she bolted *toward* Denver, not away. Totally unexpected, completely illogical." There was a pause, then he added thoughtfully, "It was a damn good strategy."

Good strategy wasn't quite how Taggart would describe it—not when he'd been chasing the elusive Ms. Genevieve Bowen for close to three months. Still, he shoved away the rude comment that sprang to mind, along with his uncharacteristic impatience. Emotion didn't have a place in the job he did as a partner in Steele Security, the business he and his brothers ran out of their home base in Denver, Colorado. The kind of work they did—hostage and fugitive recovery, personal protection, threat management, industrial security— required clear but creative thinking, situational analysis, high-stakes decision making.

Taggart regarded being cool and impartial an absolute necessity. It ought to be chiseled in stone, if you asked him—his brother Dominic's recent marriage to a wealthy debutante he'd rescued from the clutches of a ruthless Caribbean dictator notwithstanding.

He shifted his gaze from the cabin to the ancient

Ford pickup parked at the far end of it. Just because the vehicle's recent history fit with his quarry's MO—blend in, deal in cash, vanish after dropping false hints about your destination—that didn't automatically mean it was Bowen. There was still a chance she'd again eluded him—and gained the gratitude and ensuing silence of yet another needy young woman matching her general description—by giving away the truck the way she had three previous vehicles.

Only Taggart didn't think so. And not merely because his instincts were clamoring that his luck had finally turned. Because *this* time, damned if he hadn't seen her himself, bold as brass, driving out of the Morton's Grocery parking lot on the outskirts of Kalispell.

The cabin door swung open. "I've got movement," he told Gabe. "I'll catch you later." Not waiting for a reply, he disconnected and shifted the binoculars into place as a woman stepped out onto the porch that skirted the cabin.

With icy calm, he let his gaze climb her length, starting at her fleece-topped boots and moving up her slim, blue-jeaned legs, past a serviceable green parka until he arrived, at long last, at her face.

He let out a breath he hadn't known he was holding. It was her, all right. After the dozen weeks he'd spent on her trail, interviewing her friends and showing her picture around, her features were as familiar to him as his own. There was the full mouth, the straight little nose, the big dark eyes and the slightly squared chin. Her glossy brown hair, which she'd once worn in a thick braid that reached to her waist, was now cropped short and, after a number of cut-and-color transformations, back to its original color.

He frowned as something nagged at him, and then his face smoothed out as he realized he was simply surprised by how small she was. Even though his information on her included the fact that she was only five foot three, for some reason he'd expected her to appear taller.

Nevertheless, it *was* her—Ms. Genevieve Bowen, Silver, Colorado, bookstore owner and literacy booster, teen mentor, animal lover, occasional emergency foster mother. A woman so well-known for her random acts of kindness that her friends fondly referred to her as their own little Pollyanna.

Polly-pain-in-the-butt was more like it, Taggart thought, recalling the absolute futility of the past three months. Given Ms. Bowen's glorified Girl Scout reputation, and the fact that your average model citizen didn't know jack about being on the lam, he'd assumed he'd be able to track her down without breaking a sweat.

Wrong. First to his surprise and then to his exasperation—and his brothers' not-so-subtle amusement— little Genevieve had made none of the usual beginner's mistakes. Hell, she hadn't made any mistakes. Instead, she'd simply vanished, turning a job that should have been a week-long romp into a test of Taggart's cunning and perseverance.

It was just too damn bad for her that he was very, very good at his job.

That, being a methodical son of a bitch, he'd decided after losing her trail yet again to revisit all the places he'd initially pegged as being potential bolt holes for her, including her late great-uncle's northern Montana cabin where she and her brother—who was currently being held without bail on charges of capital murder—had spent several long-ago summers.

And that, in an unpredictable turn of luck, he'd just happened to pull into that grocery store lot at the same time she'd been pulling out. Otherwise, he not only would have missed her, he'd have once again struck the cabin off his list for now and most likely spent another few weeks fruitlessly trying to locate her.

Instead, he'd called in the pickup's plates to Gabe and followed her back here, managing to remain undetected only because he'd been pretty damn sure where they were going. Once again, what had been good for him had been bad for her.

But then, Genevieve hadn't exactly had a banner year, what with her brother's arrest for killing James Dunn, his client's only son; her own unwanted role as the prosecution's key witness and her dumb-ass decision to flee rather than testify.

Because now she was *his*. With a distinct surge of possessiveness, he watched as she reached the truck, keeping the binoculars trained on her vivid face as she retrieved a bag of groceries and trekked back the way she'd come.

Suddenly, just as she reached the stairs that led up to the cabin's railed porch, she stopped. Swiveling her head, she looked straight at him.

Taggart knew damn well she couldn't see him. Still, he felt her gaze like a lover's touch. Rooted in place, he forgot to breathe, stunned as his skin prickled and he felt the oddest tug of recognition....

It seemed like an eternity before she looked away, gave the rest of the clearing a careful once-over, then squared her shoulders and went quickly up the trio of steps. Pausing under the wide overhang that sheltered the door, she abruptly glanced one last time directly at the spot where he stood before she disappeared inside.

Annoyed, he blew out his pent-up breath, asking himself what the hell had just happened. Just who did she think she was? Some sort of psychic? His long-lost soul mate?

Yeah, right. It'd be a cold day in hell when he started believing in that kind of delusional mumbo jumbo.

Jaw clenched, he stowed the binoculars and surged into motion. Carefully hugging the shadow of the trees, he began to work his way toward the back of the cabin, his powerful body making short shrift of the thigh-high snowdrifts.

Enough cat and mouse. It was time to take her down.

Genevieve set the bag of groceries on the kitchen counter. Chilled despite the warmth of her parka, she rubbed her arms and did her best to dispel her lingering sense of unease.

Try as she might to downplay it, she'd had the most uncomfortable sensation of being watched while she was outside. It had been sharp, overwhelming, eerie— as palpable as an actual touch. Alarm had flickered along her spine; gooseflesh had erupted on her arms and prickled the nape of her neck.

She'd felt a powerful urge to run.

That's what you get for staying up late last night reading Stephen King. Keep it up, and the next thing you know, you'll start to think the trees are alive. Or that a mutant squirrel is coming to get you....

A wry little smile tugged briefly at the corners of her mouth. Okay. So maybe she was a wee bit jumpy. It wasn't really surprising, not when her stop in town to get supplies had filled her with such conflicting feelings.

Typical of her current existence, she'd been scared to death that someone might recognize her while also wishing fervently that she might see a familiar face. Which was not only illogical and contradictory, but also highly improbable since the last time she'd been in the area for more than a night she'd been barely fifteen, nearly half the age she was now.

Still, she knew she was taking a chance by coming here. *How to Vanish without a Trace,* the book that had been her bible these past months, warned against seeking out known and familiar places.

And yet… Not only was she running dangerously low on money, but she'd changed her identity so many times they were starting to run together. She needed a break—just a week or maybe two—to rest and regroup. And surely, after all this time, anyone still looking for her would have written this place off.

Lord, she hoped so, she thought, turning to glance fondly at the cabin's simple interior. The structure was a standard, open-concept A-frame. Toward the back, an L-shaped kitchen occupied one side, while the bathroom and a sleeping area with a massive built-in bed occupied the other, the two areas separated by a narrow stairway that led up to a small loft.

A bank of windows stretched across the cabin's front, divided by a floor-to-ceiling native-stone fireplace equipped with a glass-fronted heat insert. Although the oversized navy couch, the trio of maple occasional tables and the pair of padded rocking chairs were new, chosen by the property management company she'd hired when the place had passed to her and her brother, they had clean, uncluttered lines, like the old furniture she remembered, and were placed to make the most of the sweeping view of the surrounding peaks.

If she closed her eyes, she could almost believe it was fourteen years ago and that any second her great-uncle Ben would come clattering through the door, an adoring twelve-year-old Seth dogging his heels. The two would snatch away whatever book she happened to be reading—her little brother complained that Genevieve was *always* reading—and tug her out on the deck to see the sunset or watch an eagle soaring overhead.

Except that Uncle Ben had been gone more than a decade, the last to pass of the quintet of elderly relatives who'd done the best they could to provide their great-niece and great-nephew with some occasional normalcy. While Seth…

Her heart clenched at the memory of the last time she'd seen her brother. Dressed in an orange jumpsuit, his hands weighed down with shackles, Seth's normally easygoing expression had been closed and implacable as he faced her through the mesh divide of the visitors' room of the Silver County Jail. "No. No way, Gen," he'd said flatly. "You go into court and refuse to testify, they're going to throw you in jail, too."

"But—"

"*No.* It's bad enough that you're probably going to

lose your house—and for what? To pay an attorney who thinks I'm guilty? But I swear to God I'll confess before I'll let you sacrifice your freedom."

"Seth, don't be foolish—"

"I'm not kidding. It's a slam dunk I'm going to be convicted." His voice had been even, almost uninflected, but his eyes had been so defeated it had taken all her strength not to lay her head down on the scarred counter between them and weep. "The best thing you can do is accept that I'm a lost cause and just…move on."

As if, Genevieve thought fiercely now. The mere thought of giving up on her little brother was inconceivable. They'd never known their father, and it had been just the two of them ever since their mother had abandoned them for good when Genevieve was ten and Seth was seven. She certainly wasn't about to sit back now and do nothing while he was punished for something he hadn't done. Any more than she would play a part, however unwilling, in making him appear guilty.

So, after considerable agonizing, she'd decided to run. It was far from a perfect solution—she accepted that eventually she'd have to pay for defying the court—but so far, at least, she'd done what she'd set out to. The trial had been delayed, buying Seth some time. And there was always a chance that one of the dozens of people she'd written to over the past three months— policemen, attorneys, private investigators, her congressman—might actually decide to do what she'd begged and look into the case.

In the meantime, she was doing okay. Sure, she was lonely—just as *How to Vanish* warned, the hardest part of disappearing wasn't constructing a new identity or not leaving a paper trail or even not staying too long in any one place.

The hardest part was having no one to talk to. She couldn't count the number of times during the course of a day that she longed to hear a familiar voice or see a familiar face. As much as she missed home, what she missed even more was someone to confide in, someone she could trust.

Still, as long as she had her books, her freedom and her sincere belief that if she just continued to insist on Seth's innocence somebody somewhere would eventually listen, she could survive anything.

Uh-huh. Except for that killer squirrel that's lurking outside, just waiting to get you.

Well, really. What was she going to do? Let herself be controlled by a nonexistent bogeyman, animal or otherwise? Crawl under the bed, cover her eyes and hide?

She drew herself up. Heck, no. She had enough legitimate worries without letting her imagination into the act.

Before she could lose her nerve, she zipped up her parka, strode to the door and flung it open. Marching outside, she caught her breath as a blast of frigid air swept over her, but she didn't falter. Planting herself at the top of the stairs, she scanned the clearing one more time, determined to put an end to her foolish fears. She scoured the snow for telltale footprints and searched the shadows at the base of the pines for anything out of place.

Nothing. Yet she still had the strangest feeling....

Determined to be thorough and be done with this once and for all, she turned and marched out onto the large, prow-shaped section of the deck that jutted from the cabin's front. Again she looked and listened, but there wasn't a thing to suggest another human presence. There was just a glint of sun on snow, the intermittent call of a hawk and the whisper of the wind sighing through the surrounding trees.

See? There's nobody here but you.

Blowing out a breath, she forced her stiff shoulders to relax. Everything was fine. She and her memories were the only ones here. And once she had the rest of her things out of the truck and got started on the soup she planned to make for dinner, she'd feel even better. She turned and took a step toward the stairs.

Like a ghost come to life, a man materialized out of the shadows of the overhang.

Her heart slammed to a stop along with her feet as she stared at him, the blood suddenly roaring in her ears.

Like her, he was dressed for the weather in a parka, boots and jeans. But that was where all similarity ended. He was huge, six foot four at least, with powerful legs and shoulders like a linebacker's. His hair was coal-black, cropped close to his head, and his hooded eyes were a pale, icy green.

His face was all angles, with a slash of high cheekbones, a straight blade of a nose, a stubborn chin and firm lips set in a straight, uncompromising line.

He looked dangerous as hell, and Genevieve hadn't stayed free for three months without learning to trust her instincts.

Whirling, she ran for her life.

Two

Well, hell.

Feeling a distinct stab of annoyance, Taggart launched himself after little Ms. Bowen, who appeared to be operating under the delusion that now that he'd found her, he might actually let her get away.

He swallowed a snort. There was about as much chance of that as of him dancing in the Denver Ballet.

She might be fast, but he was faster. Not to mention bigger, stronger and trained—by the US Army Rangers—to take down considerably tougher, rougher members of society than Genevieve would ever be.

Although he had to admit, closing this case was going to make his week. Hell, who was he kidding? It was going to make his *year*.

Catching up to her with ease, he tackled her, hauling her close as they reached the edge of the deck, crashed into the railing, flipped over the top and plunged toward the snowbank below.

Instinctively—he wanted to take her into custody, not put her in the hospital, damn it—he twisted, taking the brunt of the impact as they slammed to the ground. He winced as his hip struck a rock and he heard a distinct crunch of plastic as his cell phone bit the dust. Then he winced again as the back of Bowen's head slammed into his collarbone.

Baring his teeth at the pain, he loosened his grip a fraction, only to bite out a curse as his captive drove her heavily booted heels into his shins at the same time as she punched him hard in the stomach with one sharp little elbow.

That did it. Setting his jaw, he locked his legs around hers and tightened the grip he had on her midriff. "Knock it *off.*"

"Let go of me!" she countered. "Let go of me this instant or—" her voice wavered as he increased the pressure on her solar plexus, making it impossible for her to get a deep breath "—I swear…you'll—you'll be—sorry—"

She was threatening *him?* Unbelievable. The woman clearly had more nerve than sense. He tightened his hold even more. "Pay attention, lady. I'm in charge now. You do what I tell you. Understand?"

He waited a beat for her to answer.

When she didn't, he increased the pressure until she couldn't breathe at all, knowing from experience that the more he could dominate and demoralize her now, the less likely she'd be to give him trouble on their return trip to Colorado. *"Understand?"*

A whimper escaped her throat. "Yes," she finally gasped. "Yes!"

"Good." Satisfied, he loosened his hold, dumped her unceremoniously onto her side and climbed to his feet.

Knocking the snow from his pants, he considered her as she lay sprawled in the snow. With her shiny mop of hair, her eyes squeezed shut so that her inky lashes shadowed her smooth cheeks, her mouth trembling each time she took a greedy gulp of air, she looked small and defenseless, almost childlike.

Except that thanks to their recent tussle, the lush curve of her ass and the soft swell of her breasts were imprinted on his brain, leaving him in no doubt she was a thoroughly grown-up female.

And a treacherous one at that, he reminded himself, his shins throbbing annoyingly from where she'd kicked him.

"Get up," he ordered.

She drew in one last shuddering breath, then opened her eyes. He watched her struggle to control her fear, and felt a grudging admiration as she willed herself to present a semblance of calm.

She pushed herself upright, watching him warily. "What do you want with me?" she demanded.

"I work for Steele Security. James Dunn's parents hired us to find you."

"Find *me?*" She widened her dark eyes in an excellent imitation of surprise. "But why would—"

"Forget it. I know who you are, *Genevieve*—so whatever you're trying to sell, I'm not buying. Now, get up."

She stayed where she was. Probing the back of her head, she winced and dropped her gaze. "I will. It's just—I'm a little dizzy."

He took a threatening step forward. "Now."

She flinched and threw up her hands. "Okay, okay!" Brushing the hair out of her eyes, she gave a defeated sigh and reached up for assistance getting to her feet.

Normally he'd have taken a step back and left her to deal on her own. But not only were her lips trembling again, but her outstretched hand was suddenly shaking, too.

With a faint, exasperated sigh of his own, he reached down. Her delicate palm slid across his calloused, much larger one. Yet the instant he tightened his grip, damned if her other hand didn't swing up and clamp around his wrist. With surprising strength for such a little bit of a thing, she threw her weight backward, yanking him forward at the same time she drew up her legs and lashed out.

She was quick, he'd give her that. Luckily, however, he was quicker. He threw himself sideways, and instead of her boot heels catching him in the groin as she'd obviously intended, they thudded heavily into his right thigh.

The blow caught him squarely in the femoris muscle and hurt like hell. Off balance, he stumbled, his leg twanging as if comprised of overstretched guitar strings.

It was all the advantage his adversary needed. Giving him one final kick, this time in the knee, she rolled away, sprang to her feet and bolted toward the trees.

"Son of a bitch." He couldn't remember the last time

he'd lost his temper, having learned early on to regard intense emotion of any kind as the enemy.

Yet suddenly he was on the verge of being genuinely pissed.

He tore after her. Catching up with her handily, he snagged the neck of her parka in his fist, then set his feet and yanked, jerking her off her feet.

"Let go of me! I'm warning you—" Twisting, she struck out at him, and damned if one of her flailing hands didn't connect with a glancing blow to his mouth.

If he'd been Gabe, he probably could've soothed her with a few reasonable words. If he'd been Dominic or Cooper, he most likely could've charmed her into submission. But he had neither a gift for reassurance nor a way with women and he was sick and tired of being used as a punching bag.

"That's *it!*" Ducking his head, he caught her by the thighs and tossed her over his shoulder.

This can't be happening, Genevieve thought, kicking and squirming as her captor strode effortlessly through the snow. It wasn't right. This big, scary-looking stranger with his hard body and shuttered eyes couldn't just appear in her life, overpower her and drag her back to Silver.

Somebody obviously forgot to tell him that, though, because that seems to be exactly what he's doing. And you can pummel and threaten him all you want, but he's still going to be able to overpower you.

It was clearly time to change tactics. She was no match for him physically, which meant if she was going to have a chance at escape, she was going to have to outwit him—easier said than done when she was hanging upside down, the blood rushing to her head, her stomach jouncing painfully against his hard shoulder with every step.

She thought hard for a moment, then blew out a breath, forced herself to quit struggling and went limp.

Nothing happened for what felt like an eternity. Finally, however, she felt the faintest hesitation in her adversary's long, effortless stride. "You all right, Bowen?" he asked.

"No." Sounding weak and pathetic didn't require any effort. "If you don't put me down, I'm going to lose my breakfast."

Darned if he didn't shrug, lifting and lowering her with a hitch of his shoulder as if she weighed nothing. "Tough."

"But—"

"*No.*" He paused for a beat. "And if you get sick on me, you're gonna regret it."

His low voice held just enough menace that she believed him totally. Even so, he couldn't really expect her to control something like that—could he?

Deciding she'd prefer not to find out, she swallowed. Hard. "What—what's your name?"

He was silent so long she didn't think he was going to answer. Finally, he said, "Taggart."

"Is that your first name or your last?"

"Just Taggart's all you need to know."

Nobody was ever going to accuse him of being a chatterbox. She gulped as he hefted her a little higher. "Okay, Just—" She started to call him Just Taggart, then thought better of it. Antagonizing him more than she already had couldn't be wise. "Listen, please? I'm not rich, but whatever you're getting paid, I'll double it if you'll let me go."

"No."

"Then how about if you just put off taking me back for say…a week?" Surely she could find a way to escape in that space of time. "We can stay here. You'll still be doing your job, but I'll pay you, too, and I've got lots of supplies and—"

"No."

"Then what about a day? Just one day. Surely twenty-four hours can't matter—"

"Not gonna happen, Genevieve." Without warning, he dumped her on her feet next to the truck. Towering over her, he gave her a quick once over, his ice-green eyes impossible to read. Then he caught her by the shoulder and spun her around. "Now shut up, keep your hands where I can see them and spread your legs." Planting a palm between her shoulder blades, he gave her a nudge.

She had barely enough time to throw up her hands and brace herself against the fender before his big, hard hands were on her. They skimmed impersonally down her arms and skated over her back, breasts and sides, then slipped downward to explore her legs and thighs.

Humiliation painted her cheeks with fire as he patted her hips, then gave a huff of satisfaction as he encountered the car keys she'd zipped into her coat pocket. Before she could voice a protest, he took possession of them, then resumed his exploration. By the time he finished, she was shaking all over from the indignity of his touch.

"Okay," he murmured, reaching around her to open the truck door. "Get in."

"But my things—"

"Are in back where you left them."

"But I can't just leave!" She twisted around to face him. "What about the cabin? The fire's going and I've got groceries sitting out and—"

"I'll arrange for somebody to come and close things up."

"Okay, but—but we really shouldn't take the truck. The heater's shot and the brakes aren't reliable and the lights don't always work and it'll be dark soon—"

"No sweat. My rig is parked on the next track south."

"But—"

"Enough." The look he sent her was frigid enough to flash-freeze boiling water. "You can babble until hell freezes over, but I still plan to be back in Colorado—with you in custody—this time tomorrow. Got it?"

She thought about Seth, about his threat to confess rather than allow her to forfeit her own freedom and felt a spurt of desperation. Surely there had to be some way to reach this man, some way to change his mind. "I know you have a job to do, but you have to understand. I can't go back. Not yet."

"Oh, yeah. You can. You are."

"Please! Just listen. My brother's innocent. But if you take me back, he'll feel obligated to try and protect me and—"

"Get in the truck, Bowen." He took a step closer, the toe of one big boot bumping her smaller one.

It took every ounce of her courage, but she stood her ground. "Damn it, Taggart, if you'll just listen—"

"No." With a speed that was surprising for a man his size, he caught her under the arms and boosted her onto the seat. Then he gripped her right arm with one hand, reached under his coat with the other and the next thing she knew, he was slapping a handcuff around her wrist.

"Don't!" She tried to twist away but it was too late as he snapped the other bracelet around the door handle. "Surely that's not—"

"I don't like surprises when I'm driving."

Frightened, furious, she watched helplessly as he slammed the door and headed around to the driver's side of the truck.

Think, she ordered herself as he slid the seat back as far as it would go to accommodate his mile-long legs and climbed inside.

Taking a firm grip on her emotions, Genevieve turned to face him. "I don't have much money, most of it went to pay for Seth's attorney, but you can have my house. I'll sign it over. My business, too. I'll—I'll give you anything you want. Just name it."

For a moment it was as if he hadn't heard her. Then he abruptly twisted on the seat and leaned over so that only inches separated them. His cool compelling gaze slid from her hair to her eyes to her mouth, then flicked back up. "Anything?" His eyes gleamed dangerously.

He was so close she could see each individual inky whisker shadowing his cheeks, as well as a faint, razor-thin scar that cut through one corner of his hard, unsmiling mouth.

Her stomach dropped and what was left of the moisture in her mouth dried up. She told herself not to be a fool, to say, "Yes, of course, whatever it takes," but when she parted her lips, the words wouldn't come out. "I—I—"

His head dipped even closer. Swallowing hard, she squeezed her eyes shut, her heart slamming into her throat as his hair—cool and unexpectedly soft—tickled against her cheek.

Then he abruptly straightened and she felt the pressure as he dragged her seat belt across her waist. Her eyes flew open as he jammed the end into the clasp with a distinctive click.

He sent her a mirthless smile as their gazes meshed. "Yeah. I didn't think so. Which is just as well, since the only thing I want from you—" he fastened his own seat belt and slapped the truck into Reverse "—is your word that you won't give me any more trouble."

Embarrassed, insulted, affronted, disgusted—Genevieve couldn't decide what she felt most. "Go to hell."

He gave a faint sigh. "Too late. Already been there, done that," he murmured. Depressing the clutch, he backed the vehicle out of its slot. He shifted, straightened the wheel and began to guide the truck down the narrow, tree-lined track that led to the road.

The deer came out of nowhere. One second there was nothing in front of them but an unobscured ribbon of white. In the next, a rangy young stag bounded squarely into their path, its dun-colored hide seeming to fill the entire windshield.

"Watch out!" Genevieve cried as Taggart wrenched the wheel to the left. He hit the brakes and the old Ford bucked wildly, fishtailed across the snowy ground and slammed driver's side first into an enormous evergreen tree.

Taggart's head hit the door frame with a sickening crunch.

Genevieve watched with a mixture of awe and horror as he slumped, his big body suddenly as limp as a rag doll's. *Dear God, what if he's dead?*

Fast on the heels of that thought came another. *Dear God. What if he's not?*

Three

Taggart surfaced slowly.

As he did, several things seemed noteworthy. One was that his head felt as if a stake were being driven through it.

The other was that somebody—a woman, judging from her soft voice and even softer hands—was touching him. "Come on now," she murmured, her husky voice tickling along his spine while her fingers sifted featherlight through the hair at his temple. "It's time to quit fooling around. Wake up now. I know you can do it."

She knew he could do it. Her faith gave him pause. The first and last female to unswervingly believe in him had been his mother. Yet he knew damn well that the woman murmuring to him wasn't **Mary Moriarity Steele**.

She smelled entirely different, for one thing, like sunshine and soap instead of lavender and baby powder. Plus her hands were smaller and her voice was lower. Besides, his mother had been gone…

How long? Drawing a blank, he struggled to punch through the fog hazing his brain. For a frustrating moment his mind remained shrouded and sluggish. Then the knowledge abruptly bubbled up.

Twenty years. She'd died twenty years ago last month, the anniversary of her passing falling on the day after his thirty-third birthday.

What's more, with another burst of returning memory he knew that it was Genevieve Bowen who was showing him such gentle concern. He recognized her voice at the same instant the recollection of tossing her over his shoulder and heading for her truck came rushing back at him. Yet after that… Nothing.

He didn't have a single, solitary doubt who was to blame.

Marshaling his strength, he opened his eyes. He felt a perverse flicker of satisfaction as his quarry—hell, no, his *prisoner*—sucked in a startled breath and jerked back, snatching her hand away from his face.

"Genevieve." Even to his own ears, his voice sounded raspy.

"You're back."

"Yeah." He blinked, tried to make sense of the timbered ceiling above his head and failed. With a prickle of uneasiness, he realized he was lying on a bed in a room he'd never seen before.

"How do you feel?"

He told himself to focus. Okay, so his brain seemed

to be a few cards short of a full deck and he had a son of a bitch of a headache—so what? He'd survived worse. He concentrated on what he did remember and tossed out an educated guess. "The truck. There was an accident."

"Yes." She nodded. "There was a deer. In the road. You swerved to avoid it and hit a tree."

"I knew that," he lied. "What I meant was—how long have I been out?"

"You don't remember?"

"No."

A spark of something—it looked a lot like compassion except he knew damn well that couldn't be right—flared in her eyes. "You've been in and out, but mostly out, the past hour. And in case you're wondering, you're in the cabin. My great-uncle's cabin."

Of course. He glanced around, taking note of the comfortable-looking furniture, the fire dancing cheerfully behind the glass doors of a big stone fireplace, the stretch of windows looking out on the jagged Montana peaks stabbing into the sky. Bringing his gaze back to her, he wondered how she'd managed to get him inside, given that he was twice her size, then decided there was a different question he was far more curious about. "And you're still here…why?"

She was silent a moment, then gave a dismissive little shrug. "You took a pretty nasty knock to the head. I couldn't just go off and leave you. Not until I was sure you were okay."

Yeah, right. Pollyanna reputation or not, she wasn't stupid and *nobody* was that good-hearted. More likely she was tired of being hunted and, having finally come face-to-face with what she was up against—that would be *him*—had realized the futility of continuing to run.

Then again, she'd saved him a boatload of aggravation by hanging around. If she wanted to pretend she was Doris Do-right, what the hell did he care? He inclined his chin a fraction, ignoring the ensuing howl of protest from his aching head. "Thanks."

"You're welcome." Even as she took a step back, putting a little more distance between them, an uncertain smile kissed the corners of her full mouth.

He scowled as part of him that was unapologetically male whispered *pretty*. Reminding himself sharply that she was his assignment, not his date, for God's sake—and he never mixed his personal and professional lives—he stared expressionlessly at her. "Don't get the wrong idea," he said flatly as he carefully pushed himself upright. "You're still my prisoner and I'm—*what the hell?*"

Something heavy was dragging at his arm. He sensed Bowen moving even farther away as he glanced down, confounded to see that a handcuff was locked around his left wrist. What's more, the adjoining stainless-steel bracelet had been threaded through the end links of a heavy chain that had been passed around the end support of the massive built-in bed frame.

He was trapped like a wolf in a snare.

Ignoring the pounding in his head, he didn't think but acted, launching himself at his one chance at freedom.

He was within inches of grabbing her when it dawned on him that instead of bolting the way she ought to be, his nemesis was holding her ground, and a warning shrieked through his brain.

Too late. Unable to check himself, he reached the end of his tether and was damn near jerked off his feet.

The handcuff cut into his wrist. His arm felt as if it was being ripped from his shoulder. Then his momentum snapped him around and his head exploded in agony.

Gritting his teeth against the howl crowding his throat, he staggered back the way he'd come, braced himself against the bed frame and sank down onto the quilt-covered mattress.

So much for his luck having changed, he thought savagely. With a snap of her fingers, Lady Fortune had snatched away success and turned him from victor to casualty, from hunter to captive.

It was a road he'd traveled before, he reminded himself. Under far worse circumstances, with far graver consequences.

But he wasn't going to think about that. It was over. In the past. Beyond his reach to change. He needed to focus on the here and now. On Genevieve.

Locking firmly onto that single thought, he squeezed his eyes shut and forced himself to hold perfectly still as he waited for the worst of the pain to pass.

Enduring, after all, was what he did best.

"Here." Genevieve set the pill bottle and the glass of water on the nightstand, all the while keeping a wary eye on the big man hunched on the bed. "This should help."

Mindful of the terrifying show of speed and strength he'd put on just minutes earlier, she quickly stepped back out of reach. And waited.

Nothing. He continued to sit perfectly still, head slumped, eyes shut, broad shoulders rigid.

"It's ibuprofen. My first aid book says that's okay for someone in your condition."

Still no reaction. With an inner shrug, she decided that if he wanted to imitate a boulder there was nothing she could do about it. She'd give it one more try; then she was done.

"If you think a cold compress would help, let me know. The fridge hasn't been on long enough to make ice, but there's plenty of snow outside." Silence. "Hokay then, J.T." With a shrug, she started to turn away. "I'll just give you some space—"

"Don't call me that."

Turning back, she found his gaze fixed on her, his eyes hooded and impossible to read. "What?" Her response was automatic even though she knew perfectly well what he was referring to.

"J.T.," he gritted out. "Don't call me that. I don't like it."

For a second she was speechless. Of all the things she might've expected him to object to, her flippant abbreviation of Just Taggart wasn't even on the list. Still, given that she had the upper hand, she supposed she could afford to be gracious. "All right. Plain old Taggart it is then." She felt a fleeting flash of amusement as she considered what he'd say if she called him by *that* acronym.

Moving carefully, and looking as if *he* hadn't smiled about anything in years, he reached for the pill bottle and thumbed off the cap. To her dismay, he proceeded to toss back considerably more than the recommended dosage. Setting down the water glass, he eased back farther on the bed, then sliced her a sharp look. "What?"

"I—nothing." She wiped the concerned look off her face, telling herself not to be foolish. He was a grown-up, and bigger than average, and if he wanted to suck down the entire bottle of pain reliever, it was none of her business. While she obviously hadn't been ruthless enough after the accident to shove him out of the truck and abandon him to his fate, she was neither stupid nor naive enough to think anything had changed.

He was her enemy.

A crucial little fact she couldn't afford to forget, she reminded herself, turning away. Sure, she was lonely. Sure she was dying to talk openly to somebody. And yes, the sight of anyone injured or hurting tended to trigger what Seth had always claimed was her overdeveloped nurturing streak.

But she'd be grade-A certifiable, lock-me-in-the-asylum-and-throw-away-the-key crazy to let down her guard even an inch where the man on the bed was concerned.

And it wasn't only the risk he posed to her freedom, his obvious mental toughness, killer physique or ability to handle himself that she found so threatening, she mused as she walked over to the kitchen and began methodically putting away the groceries.

No, there was something else, some intangible quality he possessed that made her feel off balance and not quite herself. Something that tugged at her senses and alarmed her recently awakened sense of self-preservation all at the same time.

Uh-huh. That's called the thrill of danger, the call of

the wild, Genevieve. Women have been drawn to dangerous men like moths to the flame since the beginning of time.

Add to that the fact that he wasn't exactly ugly and it was perfectly reasonable that he inspired such conflicting feelings in her. Not that he was pretty-boy handsome. Far from it. Along with that dark hair and those pale eyes, he had the strongly sculpted, slightly ascetic face of a medieval warrior.

But she wasn't attracted to him, for heaven's sake. She absolutely was not. Even if she'd met him under different circumstances—say, when he wasn't doing his damnedest to hijack her life—he was so far from her type it wasn't even funny. He was too big, too tightly wound, too…male.

Plus he had an air of watchfulness, of being apart, that troubled her. Most people had a need to be liked, to connect with others, to smooth their path through life with at least a pretense of mutual experience or interest.

Not him. He seemed walled off, although she had a feeling she didn't question that beneath that carefully controlled surface there were strong emotions at play. Perhaps that was why, even chained and hurting, he filled the cabin with his blatantly masculine presence, making her aware of him without ever saying a word.

Why even now, as she dragged a large cast-iron pot out of the cupboard, set it on the stove and busied herself with sautéing meat and chopping vegetables for the soup, she could *feel* him watching her. Just as she'd sensed him observing her earlier.

She gave a rueful little sigh. God. What she wouldn't

give for her earlier foreboding to have been caused by a good old killer squirrel, mutant or not.

Instead, she was stuck with a much more terrifying human male.

Of course, she supposed things could have turned out worse—far worse. She'd gotten incredibly lucky with that deer. And Taggart, for all his aura of imminent threat, hadn't hurt her despite having had plenty of opportunity, not even in retaliation when she'd struck him first. In all fairness, she supposed she had to give him points for that—and consider the possibility that he was more civilized than she imagined.

"You don't really think you're going to get away with this, do you, Bowen?"

Then again, maybe not. Despite her prisoner's uninflected tone, she recognized a threat when she heard one. Which, she reflected, as she added a can of tomatoes, broth and seasonings to the meat, really did take an incredible amount of nerve given their respective situations.

"Do yourself a favor. Undo these cuffs. I swear I'll go easy on you."

Oh, right. Like she believed that. And even if it was true, what exactly did it mean—that he'd use velvet ribbon to truss her up when he delivered her back to Silver?

Rolling her eyes, she transferred the raw carrots and potatoes she'd sliced into the pot. She put the lid in place, turned down the heat on the burner and moved to the sink to wash her hands.

"Okay, I get it now. This—tying guys to your bed— is how you get your kicks."

She turned off the water and dried her hands. Surely she hadn't heard that right?

"Normally, I don't go for the Suzy Homemaker type. But I suppose I could make an exception. Of course, first I'd want to see you nak—"

She swiveled around. "Are you out of your mind? Are you *trying* to tick me off?"

Propped up against the headboard, his legs stretched out, he hitched his shoulders a scant half inch. "Got your attention, didn't I?"

"Oh, yes, you did do that." She gave a theatrical sigh. "And to think three hours ago I was actually pining for the sound of another human voice." She leveled her gaze at him. "So what is it you want to say that I just have to hear?"

"How long do you plan to keep me chained like this?"

"That depends."

"On what?"

She gave a little shrug. "A variety of things. Your health. My mood. Whether you persist in making any more objectionable personal comments."

One level black eyebrow rose. "Is that a threat?"

"More like a promise," she said sweetly.

"What am I supposed to do when I need to use the facilities?"

"Bathroom's right there." She indicated the door some four feet down the wall from the bed. "The chain will reach."

"What are you going to do?"

"There's a half bath up in the loft. Not perfect, but it'll do."

He started to scowl, then appeared to reconsider. "Look, my offer still stands. End this now, let me take you back and I'll make sure the judge knows you cooperated."

"How generous of you. But I think I'll pass. You may not understand, but as I tried to explain earlier, I don't care what the judge thinks—not about me. It's my brother who matters."

"Damn it, Bowen—"

"You know, if I were you, I really wouldn't swear at me. What's more, I'd at least *try* to be nice. Otherwise, I may forget to tell someone where you are once I'm gone."

His face hardened. "Sorry, sweetheart, but I'm not buying. If you meant to take off and leave me to rot, you'd have done it earlier. You're going to have to come up with a better threat than that."

"I don't think so." She came to a sudden decision. So he thought he could predict her behavior, did he? Well, maybe he could as concerned this particular issue—damn him—but that didn't mean she had to make it easy. It would do his character good to worry a little for a change.

Grabbing her parka off the hook near the door, she slid it on, checking her pocket to make sure the keys to his rig were still in it. "I guess I'll see you later. Or then again—maybe not."

"What the hell's that supposed to mean?" he demanded.

She smiled without humor and scooped up her purse. "You think you know everything. Figure it out." Her hand on the doorknob, she glanced back at him over her shoulder. "Oh, and just so we're clear? I wouldn't sleep with you if you came dipped in chocolate."

Without looking back, she flicked him a wave and sailed out the door.

Four

Gripping the bathroom doorjamb, Taggart glanced narrowly at the silvery twilight rapidly fading beyond the cabin windows.

Terrific. Just frigging terrific. It was getting dark and there was still no sign of Bowen.

He walked unsteadily to the bed and sank gingerly down on the edge. Careful not to jar his head, he unlaced his hiking boots and slid them off, then lay back and stretched out, letting himself stew as he scowled up at the plank ceiling overhead.

Not that he was worried. At least, not much. While he still didn't buy the concept that anyone could be as pure of heart as she was reputed to be, he was confident little Ms. Genevieve was coming back—and for reasons that had nothing to do with her supposed concern for his health.

She had, for example, gone to considerable effort putting together whatever was simmering deliciously on the stove. Why do that if she didn't plan to return to eat some of it? It sure as hell wasn't as if *he* could reach it, he thought, trying to ignore the pathetic way his mouth was watering in reaction to the rich, savory aroma.

What's more, there was no way she would've taken off without the duffel bag and the box of books that were currently parked by the door, which she must've hauled in from the truck while he was in la-la land. It would also be reckless and stupid of her to have left so late in the day without a plan—and from everything he'd seen so far she was plenty smart.

By now, she was bound to have figured out it would be a day or two before anyone would expect them to show up in Silver. It wouldn't take much additional brain power for her to realize that even when they were a no-show, an alarm most likely wouldn't be immediately raised since he was so obviously not the kind of guy to tolerate a short leash.

Which was why the prudent thing for her to do would be to remain at the cabin and take some time considering her next move.

The alternative—that she'd taken off for good—was unacceptable.

Because, damn it, he'd already searched every inch of space he could reach and hadn't found a thing he could use to pick the lock on the handcuffs. Just as he'd tested each chain link as well as the bed frame for weakness and scored a big fat zero.

So if Bowen didn't come back, short of gnawing his hand off he'd have no choice but to wait to be rescued.

The mere thought of *that* set a nerve ticking in his jaw. And not just because of the obvious humiliation factor. Or that his brothers were guaranteed to give him serious grief the second they learned he'd let an amateur—and a woman at that, for God's sake—get the drop on him. Or even because he'd be forced to start the hunt for a certain annoying little brunette all over again.

No, what was really going to rankle was that he'd have no one to blame for her decision to run but himself.

So what if he had a monster headache? So what if the past three months had been beyond frustrating? Who gave a rip that being at someone else's mercy seriously teed him off? Or that it was a well-known fact, at least in his portion of the universe, that he sucked at charming chitchat.

Only a freaking idiot would antagonize his jailer without a specific goal or a damn good reason.

Yeah, but that's precisely what you did, Ace. And you might as well admit that what really pushed you over the edge was Bowen herself. Face it. There's just something about her that rubs you the wrong way.

The ache in his head ratcheted up a notch and with a stab of impatience he realized every muscle in his body was as tightly strung as a trip wire. More than a little exasperated—control, after all, was his middle name—he blew out a pent-up breath and ordered himself to get a grip.

Okay, so being around her made him feel…itchy. As

if his skin was too small for his body. And for some inexplicable reason, probably because the blow to his head had temporarily disconnected a wire, he kept getting unwanted flashes of the way she'd felt against him, all small and soft and perfectly curved, when they'd wrestled in the snow earlier.

It didn't excuse the fact that he'd screwed up. That he'd flat-out failed the first rule of Hostage 101, which was to make your captor see you as a fellow human being. Worse, he'd let his mouth get ahead of his brain and gone out of his way to antagonize her.

And now all he could do was wait—and reflect on his numerous and varied mistakes.

So that when Bowen did return—and she *would*, by God—he'd be ready to make nice, to channel some of his brothers' winning ways with women and try to forge a bond between them, however slight.

But then, slight was all he needed. His goal, after all, wasn't to become her best friend or her lover. It was simply to get her to stick around long enough for him to regain control of the situation. To regain control of her.

He didn't have a doubt in the world he could do it. God knew, he'd faced far tougher situations doing recon missions in Afghanistan. And while the make-friends, play-nice-with-others thing wasn't going to be easy, nothing that mattered ever was.

Besides, it wasn't as if he had to share his life story with her. Or talk about anything he cared about. Like being banished as a kid to Blackhurst. Or the disaster at Zari Pass, which had put an end to his military career—and been the last time he'd allowed anyone to call him J.T.

No, his personal private business could, and would, remain just that. Personal and private.

All he had to do was be nominally civil. To offer Bowen—no, *Genevieve,* he admonished himself—the proverbial olive branch until either she lowered her guard enough for him to get the drop on her or he figured out how to free himself. As for payback…he'd see to that later.

For now, all he needed, all he wanted, he thought, finally giving in to the hammering in his head and letting his eyes drift shut against the fading light, was for this frigging headache to take a one-way hike.

And for Genevieve to be predictable for once and walk back through the door.

Nighttime fell like a heavy ebony cape.

Caught midway along the track that led to the cabin, Genevieve slowed the pickup to allow her eyes time to adjust to the swift slide from hazy dusk to inky darkness.

Despite the choppy rumble of the engine, she could hear the wind as it surged restlessly through the towering evergreens around her, making the snow-shrouded trees sway like uneasy ghosts. Overhead, a pack of marauding clouds took ever bigger bites out of the sky, obliterating the moon and swallowing stars a constellation at a time.

A shiver skated down her spine. She tried telling herself she was just chilled—she hadn't been kidding earlier when she'd told Taggart the truck's heater didn't work, and in the past ten minutes her fingers, nose and toes had started to go numb—but she knew that wasn't all it was. There was simply something spooky, a sort of bone-deep dread, that came with being alone in the dark, surrounded by an untamed wilderness, with the threat of a storm lurking in the wind.

Add to the cold and the declining weather the fact that she was tired, as much from the stressful events of the day as the three-mile hike through the snow she'd made to complete her errand, and it was no wonder she was ready to get back to the cabin.

Even if that meant having to share space with one John Taggart Steele. Whose complete name she now knew courtesy of the registration in his rig, which she'd confirmed by finally taking a look at the ID in his wallet, which she'd liberated when he'd been unconscious.

Not, she told herself hastily, that she cared what he called himself. Except for a mild curiosity about his aversion to being referred to as J.T, which, as it turned out, really were his initials, it was no skin off her nose if he went by Bozo the Clown.

What did matter was her discovery that he and the firm he worked for carried the same name. It might not be a hundred percent proof-positive, but when factored in with his relentless, self-assured personality, it made her strongly suspect that he was a principal in the enterprise rather than simply an employee.

If that was true, it was good news for her since it meant he had not just power but autonomy, and that made it a lot less likely anyone would be checking up on him anytime soon or expecting him to report in regularly.

It wouldn't be smart to count on it, however, she reflected as the truck shuddered over the last rise and the cabin came into sight. Grateful that she'd had the fore-sight to switch on the stove and porch lights before she left, she drove down the shallow hill and parked, mus-cled open the badly dented driver's-side door and headed inside, his lightweight pack slung over her shoulder.

No, she was a firm believer in hoping for the best but doing whatever was within her power to make things go her way. Which was why, she thought, as she climbed the cabin steps, retrieved the distributor cap from her pocket and dropped it with a satisfying thunk behind the wood pile, Taggart was going to have to make a trip to the auto parts store in the near future if he wanted his big black SUV to run. Of course, first he'd have to find it in the abandoned barn where she'd hidden it.

Stomping the snow off her boots, she said a sincere thank-you to the book gods for *Alan's Guide to Auto Engine Basics*. Then she pushed open the door and stepped inside, mentally straightening her spine as she braced to go another round with her less-than-charm-ing captive.

To her surprise, no sarcastic remark greeted her re-turn. Instead, except for the faint hiss and pop of the fire, the dimly lit room was eerily quiet.

Her heart stuttered. In the space of time it took her to toss away his pack and pivot toward the bed, her imagination conjured the worst possible scenario: Tag-gart had somehow gotten loose. Any second now he was going to explode out of the shadows, wrap his iron-banded arms around her and yank her against his big, hard-as-steel frame—

But no. *No*. Relief sucked the starch right out of her as she made out the solid, long-legged shape sprawled on the bed. Locking her shaking knees, she fought to regain her composure, only to abandon the effort as fear for her safety reluctantly gave way to concern for his well-being.

She felt a stir of alarm at his continuing silence. Driven to make sure he was still breathing, she crossed the room and crept as close to the bed as she dared. To her gratification, from her new vantage point she could see his chest in his gray flannel shirt rising and falling as steadily as a metronome.

The breath she hadn't known she was holding sighed out while her legs once again went as weak as spent flower stems. In need of a moment to regroup, she marshaled her strength and prepared to step away and leave him to sleep.

Before she could do more than think of retreat, up snapped Taggart's eyelashes—thick, black as the night outside and the only part of his angular face that could possibly be described as soft looking—and then she was trapped in the pale-green tractor beam of his eyes.

"Hey." For all the intensity of his gaze, his voice was as rough as a weathered board and more than a little groggy. "You're back."

"Yes."

He glanced beyond her toward the darkened windows and frowned. "What time is it?"

"A little past seven."

"Huh." He raised his unfettered hand and she prepared to lunge for safety, but he only scrubbed it across his face. "Feels later."

"It's been a long day."

"Yeah. I noticed." His hand fell away and something she couldn't define flickered in his eyes. "You had me worried."

She wondered what he expected her to say. *I'm sorry?* Not a chance. *Good, it serves you right?* Well, that might be closer to the truth, but it wasn't in her nature to gloat. Even if he so richly deserved it. She gestured toward the pack she'd deep-sixed near the door. "I brought your things."

His gaze flicked over, took note, came back again. Speculation flashed across his face, but he didn't say anything.

She cleared her throat. "How do you feel?"

"You really want to know?"

"I wouldn't have asked otherwise."

He hiked himself higher on the pillows and gave a slight shrug. "Except for my vision being blurred, my stomach churning and my head feeling like the Green Bay Packers used it for a practice ball, I'm terrific."

Well, great, she thought with a sinking feeling. He'd just described all the things her first aid book listed as indicative of a concussion. Although, the upset stomach *could* be the result of the megadose of pain reliever he'd recklessly gulped earlier….

"How about you?"

She gave a start of surprise. "How about me what?"

"You okay? No worsening aches or bruises, that sort of thing?"

"I'm fine."

"Okay. I just…" He glanced away, clearly unwilling to meet her gaze and gave another dismissive little shrug. "Somebody I once knew said the same thing after a car accident. And then… It turned out later she had some internal bleeding."

He sounded so cool and detached he might have been commenting on the weather. So why was she suddenly certain that the outcome for the "she" in question hadn't been good? And that beneath his tough-as-nails, don't-give-a-damn exterior the incident still haunted him, at least a little?

Because you're a bleeding-heart romantic with a vivid imagination, Gen. A sucker, as already noted, for anyone even the slightest bit wounded.

Uh-huh. More likely she was just a sucker, period. Because the chances were excellent that he was simply making the whole thing up, creating a fictitious person and a fictitious event in an attempt to get to her. Just as he was feigning concern for her well-being in hopes that she'd make a misstep he could use to his advantage.

And if he wasn't?

Well, that didn't matter either, she told herself firmly. Whatever the truth, she strongly doubted he'd welcome her sympathy, and she certainly didn't want *his.*

"I'm fine," she said again, turning her back on him and walking away. Tugging off her gloves, she shed her parka and hung it up, then sat down on the ottoman next to the sofa to divest herself of her boots. "Look, I realize you may not feel like it—" she pushed to her stocking feet and padded into the kitchen "—but would you be willing to try to eat something? I mean, I'll understand if you're not up for it, but it might help settle your stomach." Lifting dishes down from the cupboard, she glanced at him over her shoulder.

"I can give it a try." Shutting his eyes, he rubbed gingerly at his temple.

Well, great. Here she was, trying to ply him with food to prove that he was well enough that she could take off in the morning with a clear conscience, and he had to choose now not only to be a good sport but actually to show a hint of weakness. Annoyed, she concentrated on ladling soup, steadfastly ignoring the clink of chain behind her that was followed by the slap of the bathroom door.

Seconds later, as she was rummaging around for a tray, she heard the toilet flush, followed by the sound of the faucet coming on. Pushing the hair off her forehead, she glanced around just as Taggart reappeared, his shirtsleeves rolled up, water dotting his rugged face. Standing there, he seemed to dominate the room in a way that had nothing to do with his size.

And that was why—the only reason why—her throat suddenly felt dry.

She swallowed. "You all right?" She waited as he sat back down on the bed, stuffed a pillow behind his back and leaned against the headboard before she started toward him with his food.

"Yeah."

She stopped while she was still well out of reach. "Look, I'm just going to set this on the end of the mattress, okay? I strained the meat and vegetables out of your soup, so it's just broth, but it's still hot. One false move and you'll be wearing it, understand?"

"Relax," he rumbled. "I'm not up for a wrestling match." His gaze flicked from her to the tray she slid his way with its helping of broth, soda crackers and

7-Up, and back again, and a sort of resigned exasperation that she didn't understand flashed across his face. "For now, anyway."

Shaking her head—he really was the most perplexing man—she got her own food and carried it over to the couch.

To her surprise, she was suddenly ravenous. Grateful for once that Taggart wasn't much for small talk, she applied herself to the hearty soup and thick slice of buttered French bread she'd fixed for herself.

Yet as much as she tried to pretend she was alone in the room, she couldn't completely shake her awareness of him. Which was why she knew to the second when he was done, even before he picked up the tray and stood.

She looked up warily as he approached.

Coming as close to her as the chain would allow, he set the tray on the floor and gave it a shove in her direction with his foot. "Thanks," he said gruffly. "That was good."

"You're welcome," she murmured, feeling a twinge of surprise at his display of manners. Glancing up into his hooded green eyes, she once again found herself wondering about him.

Where did he live when he wasn't terrorizing fugitive booksellers? Was he single, divorced or—she felt an inexplicable little pang—married? Did he have kids or other family? Did he *ever* smile?

Finishing the last spoonful of her soup, she watched him retreat, then retrieved the tray, added her dishes to it and hauled everything over to the counter.

She frowned as she saw that he'd eaten every scrap

she'd served him. Suddenly wondering if maybe he felt well enough for more but pride wouldn't let him ask, she swiveled around, only to find him perched on the edge of the bed, unbuttoning his gray flannel shirt. She watched, mesmerized, as the shirt parted down the middle, then gave herself a sharp mental shake. "What are you doing?"

"Getting ready for bed." He shrugged out of the garment, exposing the sleeveless black tank beneath. The dark color was the perfect contrast to the gold-tinted olive skin stretched over an acre of to-die-for muscle that bunched and flexed with his every breath.

She swallowed. "Already? It's only eight." She wasn't sure why she was protesting; she was tired, too.

"Yeah, well, if you have to know, my head hurts." He scowled at the flannel as it dangled from the chain by the right sleeve, then shook his head and slid it away.

"Oh." In contrast to his flat stomach and ridiculously narrow hips, both faithfully delineated by the clinging black knit, his shoulders looked immense. "Of course."

"Don't worry." Oblivious to her sudden paralysis, he carefully stood and stripped off his jeans, exposing an impressive length of hairy leg between his gray wool socks and black BVDs. "I promise not to slip into a coma and die in my sleep."

Oh, God. She hadn't even thought of that, she realized, as she tried—and failed—not to stare at the impressive bulge straining the front of his clingy cotton briefs. "No. Certainly not."

To her profound thankfulness, she managed to drag her gaze away a heartbeat before he glanced her way and gave her a critical once-over of his own. His eyes, the color of new leaves in the room's soft light, narrowed. "You look beat. I'd suggest you get some rest yourself."

Their gazes meshed and for an instant she saw her surprise at his concern mirrored in his face. Then his expression closed like a slamming door and he looked away.

"Or not. Doesn't matter to me one way or the other."

His abrupt change of attitude was like a bucket of ice water, snapping her out of her distraction with his physique. A sharp retort rose to her lips, but before she could get out so much as a single word, he flipped back the covers, climbed into bed and turned his back.

Shaking her head, she walked over to the closet, yanked down the sleeping bag and extra pillow and carried them over to the sofa. Killer bod or not, she thought, as she dug her nightshirt out of her bag, Taggart was, without doubt, the most impossible, arrogant, exasperating man she'd ever met.

If she were a different kind of woman, she'd be out of here so fast tomorrow morning the draft would probably blow him against the wall.

Whether he was better or not, she mused as she washed her face and brushed her teeth in the kitchen sink.

It was therefore beyond annoying that when she climbed into her makeshift bed, she couldn't make herself forget her first aid book's warning that the first twenty-four hours after a head injury were crucial. Although she could probably safely cut that time in half for Taggart, who was harder headed than anyone she'd ever known. In the meantime, however…

She threw off the covers and climbed back out of bed to set the oven timer for two hours. In the meantime, she supposed she had no choice but to keep an eye on him.

Slipping back into the sleeping bag a moment later, she switched off the light and tried to settle into sleep. Only to have Taggart's image—bare legged, broad chested, unmistakably, blatantly male—promptly muscle its way into her mind. She fought to cast it out, but like the man himself, it obstinately refused to leave.

She huffed out a heartfelt sigh.

It was going to be a long night.

Five

Taggart jolted awake.

Muscles flexed, he braced for attack, his heart pounding painfully in the half second before reality rushed in and he remembered where he was.

The mountains. Montana. In a cabin. With Genevieve.

He sagged back against the mattress. Squeezing his eyes shut, he willed away the images crowding him of another ink-black night, of another set of mountains in a country half a world away, where he'd found himself in a nightmare from which there'd been no escape.

Don't go there, he ordered himself. Think about something, anything else. The trip to Africa you've always meant to make. How pissed Dom is going to be when he finds out there's a Steele Security pool on how long it'll take him to make us all uncles. Or—what the hell—think about...Genevieve. Even she has to be a better choice than anything that pertains to Dominic's sex life.

Genevieve. Who, judging by the kitchen clock that showed it was coming up on 2:00 a.m., would soon be joining him for what would be the third of their bedside encounters tonight.

"Taggart?" she'd whisper, after she tumbled out of bed and flipped on the light above the stove so she could see to switch off the trusty oven timer. "You awake?"

"Oh, yeah," he'd answer, having learned the hard way that ignoring her would earn him a jab with the broom.

"Do you know who you are? Where you are?"

"Yeah, Genevieve, I do." Suppressing a sigh, he'd rattle off the desired information since he'd also discovered she wouldn't leave him alone until he did. It was galling to admit, but it really did seem she was hell-bent on doing what was best for him. And since somewhere in one of her damn books she'd read that periodic checks were necessary to ensure he didn't slip into a coma, interrogating him every few hours appeared to be her mission for the night.

Even though it was obvious she was exhausted. That she was finding it harder as the hours passed to shake off the steadily increasing cold. Although he supposed, in light of her persistent death grip on the broom, that at least part of the reason for her shivering might be that on some level she sensed the growing danger of poking at him as if he were a caged bear.

Oh, not for the reason she no doubt supposed—that as adversaries, for one of them to win the other had to lose. Although that was true.

But because the longer he lay in the dark and the more tired he became, the greater the likelihood that sometime in the next few hours she was going to startle him out of a sound sleep.

And God help them both, he couldn't predict how he might react or what he might do, whether in a moment of sleep-fogged confusion he might surge up off the bed and go for her throat.... That uncertainty was why he always slept alone, and always kept more than one light on. It was the same reason he'd forced himself accept that he'd never marry. Much less find the sort of blazing happiness Dom and Lilah had—

The timer sounded, shattering the silence. Even though he'd expected it, he couldn't stop the way his pulse spiked and his muscles jumped. It was a testament to the deteriorating state of his nerves, he realized. His gut twisting with self-disgust, he shifted onto his side and latched onto the only distraction available.

With a rustle of fabric and a harsh whine of her sleeping bag's metal teeth, Genevieve emerged from her cocoon on the couch. Backlit by the glow from the fireplace, her hair gleamed, as shiny as a child's. There was nothing childlike about the body momentarily revealed in silhouette as she stood, however. The upward tilt to her breasts, the lissome curve where her waist nipped in, the delicate dip at the small of her back that flared into a tight little rear end that would fit perfectly in his hands....

"Taggart?" Yawning, she pushed the thick, silky tendrils of her hair off her face and glanced in his direction.

Unsure why he did it, except that the sight of her and the undeniable response of his body made it even harder to decide what to do about the situation, he closed his eyes and feigned sleep.

He sensed more than heard her sigh. Then came the muted thump of her feet as she crossed the floor, the click of the oven light and the merciful return to relative silence as she switched off the buzzer.

Except for his slow, measured breathing, he lay perfectly still.

"Hey, come on." He heard the faint swish as she picked up the broom, felt the air around him stir at her approach. "Say something."

He forced himself not to react to the gentle poke in the shoulder.

"I know you're awake." She was quiet for a moment, then prodded him again moving closer. "Damn it, Taggart, this isn't funny." The first faint note of panic sounded in her voice. "It's cold out here and—"

Without warning, he snatched at the broom handle and yanked.

He wasn't sure who was more surprised. Him, since he didn't know what he was planning to do until he did it. Or Genevieve, who was so stunned she forgot to let go until it was too late.

With a startled shriek, she toppled forward into his waiting arms. There was a second's stunned silence as they lay face-to-face, bodies intimately nestled together, gazes locked.

A second after that, she started to struggle, kicking

and thrashing and letting him know in impressively graphic terms exactly what she thought of him.

Face set, Taggart took it as long as he could. Then, not knowing what else to do, he took a grip on the chain, rolled her beneath him and silenced her the only way he could.

Catching her flailing hands, he pressed them into the bed, lowered his head and covered her mouth with his own.

Genevieve gave a choked cry as Taggart molded his hard lips to her softer ones. His big, muscular body was hot and heavy as he pinned her to the bed, and there was no doubt, as he hitched himself higher and increased the heated pressure against her mouth, that he was all man.

Whatever she'd expected, it wasn't…this. Never in her wildest dreams would she have imagined someone so closely guarded could kiss with such reckless abandon.

But oh, he could. And though his embrace was raw and unyielding, it was also the most exciting thing she'd ever experienced.

Are you out of your mind? she asked herself hazily. You barely know him. And what you do know, you don't like. And even if you were the sort of woman to jump into bed with a big, brooding, disagreeable stranger, this one should be your very last choice.

Chained and injured, he was a threat. Up close and on the mend he was guaranteed trouble.

Yet as she'd already acknowledged, her fear of him wasn't physical. And really, what could he do? The key to the handcuffs was across the room in her pants pocket.

She told herself she ought to resist anyway. She should press her lips together, hold herself rigid, avert her head, do whatever she could to make it clear she didn't want this or him.

Except…it would be a lie—and she knew it. Which she proved when he slid his hands from her wrists to entangle their fingers, and instead of trying to escape, she held onto him with all her strength.

She could tell herself anything she chose, but the fact was her body was on fire. Hard as it was to admit, she'd never wanted anyone the way she wanted John Taggart Steele.

The realization was staggering. Stupefying. Sex had never impressed her much. Her first time had been quick, awkward and had left her feeling exposed, empty and dissatisfied. A handful of subsequent encounters hadn't been much better. When her last experience had ended with a very nice man regretfully informing her she lacked whatever it took to achieve satisfaction, she'd swallowed her hurt and humiliation and decided he was probably right.

She'd certainly never believed herself capable of the kind of breathless need that was blowing through her now like a hurricane.

But oh, wonder of wonders, she burned to wrap herself around Taggart and soak him up. She ached to stroke and taste, to burrow even closer. She wanted—oh, how she wanted—to explore every hot, powerful inch of him.

Never had she been so aware of a man. With his weight bearing down on her, she could feel the ridges of his washboard abs, the slabs of his pectoral muscles, the sinew roping his heavy thighs, the thick, solid proof of his arousal.

She probably ought to be alarmed by all that hot flesh and blatant masculinity pressed against her.

Instead, she felt a fierce gratification. And a desperate desire to experience more. Much more.

The realization stole what was left of her breath along with the last of her caution. When the tip of his tongue seared the seam of her mouth—probing, promising, demanding—she parted her lips and drank him in.

He groaned and thrust his tongue deeper. He tasted darkly exotic, his sheer, overpowering maleness as foreign to her as uncharted territory. Her head went light, as if she'd just chugged a bottle of champagne. For the first time in her life she understood the term *drunk with desire,* as deep down at her core, a liquid flame sparked and caught fire.

Desperate to touch him, she tugged, trying to liberate her hands.

She heard his breathing hitch, felt a tremor rack the big hard body molded to her own. Then, without warning, he released her and rocked up on his forearms, the abrupt movement sliding his cotton-covered arousal along the slick, aching cleft of her sex. "Shit." He jerked away.

Her eyes flew open. Staring up at his shadowed face, she saw his jaw clench and his lips compress and realized in an instant of absolute clarity that he'd misinterpreted her attempt to free herself. For a moment she couldn't think what to do. And then from somewhere came an answer: Take a chance. Show some courage. Tell him what you want.

Latching on to the advice, she reached up, buried her fingers in the cropped thickness of his hair and tugged. "Don't stop," she whispered, skimming her fingertips over the hard planes of his face. "I want this. I want *you*." She stroked the pad of her thumb across the unyielding line of his lips. "Please."

"You don't know what you're asking for," he said flatly.

"You're wrong." It was her first, her only, lie. "I know exactly."

"No. You don't. Trust me."

"That's just it—I do. I trust you to give me what I want. What I need." Guided by desperation, her fingers found their way under the hem of his shirt. She looked directly at him as she drew her hands up the firm, hot flesh of his back.

She explored the sleek muscle that bracketed his spine, then pressed her fingers into the glorious breadth of those velvet-over-steel shoulders. Slowly, languidly, she worked her way down, kneading gently when she reached the small of his back.

He gazed impassively down at her. Her stomach clenched as she realized she didn't have a clue what was going on behind the guarded green of his eyes. Dampening her kiss-tender lips, she tried once more to get through to him. "I want you. Don't make me beg. Please, John."

He flinched at her use of his name. He stared at her for a long, endless second, then a nerve jumped in the hollow of his cheek. "Damn you, Genevieve," he rasped as his control shattered like a dropped pane of glass.

With a savage curse that would have frightened her

under any other circumstance, he rolled away and off the bed. Towering over her in the darkness, his body outlined by the glimmering firelight, he tore off his T-shirt, swore briefly as it got hung up on the chain, then abandoned it to shuck off his underwear.

She barely had time to feel her stomach jump with nervous anticipation before he was on her. Dragging her up, he yanked her nightshirt over her head and tossed it away. Then he laid her down, pinning her in place with his free hand splayed lightly across her throat.

"Is this what you want?" He lowered his head and his mouth whispered like molten fire along the vulnerable underside of her jaw. "*Is it?*"

"Yes." She swallowed, stunned anew by how incredibly exciting it was to be touched by him. "Oh, yes."

"Yeah, well… We'll see about that." Despite his sardonic tone, he was exquisitely gentle as he brushed his lips down her throat and nuzzled the notch of her collarbone, then plunged lower.

She gasped as the cool silk of his hair tickled the undersides of her breasts. She gasped again as he slipped his hands under her, gripped the mounds of her bottom and lifted, the chain making a clinking noise with the movement.

Squeezing her eyes shut, she shivered as his lips grazed the hollow of her hip. "Your skin's so damn soft." He nuzzled her, unhurriedly exploring her with his mouth as he made his way toward her navel, then zeroed in on the shallow indentation and pressed a single suggestive kiss to it.

When he finally lifted his head to stare up at her with hot-eyed intensity, her whole body was throbbing and she was shivering violently—and this time not from the cold.

She felt…dazed—by the way he seemed to regard her as a feast to be savored, by his continuing display of bone-melting patience. By her body's riotous response.

He slid higher, dragging his metal tether in his wake and cupped her breast. His long fingers felt deliciously hot against her cooler flesh, and delight flared along her nerve endings. She felt poised on the edge of something big even as she tensed, expecting him to squeeze her already throbbing nipples.

A jolt of surprise rippled through her as he lowered his head and gently rubbed his beard-roughened cheek against her instead. Surprise quickly transformed into excitement as he licked a path along the tender crease where her breast met the top of her midriff.

Enthralled, mesmerized and just a touch alarmed by the power of the wave of need crashing through her, she wondered what unexpected thing he'd do next.

She didn't have to wait to find out. Shifting, he unhurriedly moved higher to trace a circle around her aching nipple with his tongue.

A rough sound of pleasure rumbled in his chest. With infuriating slowness he dampened the pebbled crest, then blew a soft stream of air over the supersensitive area. He paused as she inhaled sharply, leaned in, gently raked her with his teeth.

Then he clamped his mouth around her straining flesh and sucked. Hard.

Her world exploded. Back bowing, she dug her nails into the solid anchor of his hard shoulders and held on for dear life as pleasure pierced her like a thunderbolt. "Oh, oh, *oh!*"

Taggart couldn't believe it. He felt Genevieve coming apart, heard the shocked surprise in her voice as the climax took her, and his own body quivered like an overstrung bowstring with the need for release.

She was just so damn responsive. All her little moans and whimpers and shakes and shivers were making him wild—and that was before the stunning discovery that he could make her come just by feasting on her pert, pretty breasts.

He knew he wasn't going to be able to wait much longer to be inside her. But he also knew that if he didn't rein himself in, didn't take some time to get a firmer grip on the need pounding through him, he could hurt her, and he was damned if he'd take that chance.

He blew out a breath as her body finally quieted and she slumped back onto the mattress like a rag doll. Releasing the velvet plumpness of her nipple, he ignored the greedy urge to knee her thighs apart and plunge himself deep into her slippery tightness.

Fighting for control, he shifted onto his side, thrust the chain out of his way, propped himself on one elbow above her and prepared to drive himself crazy just a little longer, telling himself he couldn't go wrong with kissing her.

He started to lower his head, only to check his movement as her eyes opened.

"Oh." She stared up at him, her gaze luminous. "That was…" She exhaled shakily. "That was wonderful, John."

The last time he'd been called by his first name he'd

been thirteen; he'd stubbornly seen to it that it was buried along with his mother. Oddly enough, however, now that he was past the first shock, it sounded right coming from Genevieve's lips.

Yet he couldn't bring himself to say so. Couldn't imagine admitting that for reasons he didn't understand she'd been able to blow past the defenses he'd spent two decades perfecting.

It seemed better just to concentrate on the physical. Safer. Smarter. "We're not done." His voice sounded rough, even to him.

"No." She ran her hand up his arm, rubbed her palm against his biceps.

"So tell me what you want. What else turns you on."

Her hand stilled. She wet her lips. "You."

"Me what?"

"You. You turn me on. I never...I didn't expect—" As light as a whisper, she trailed the tip of her index finger down his cheek. "More than anything—" Her hand shook almost imperceptibly as she sketched the shape of his upper lip "—I want you inside me."

Five words. Five mind-blowing little words and his hands—hands that could defuse a bomb without a quiver, hold a rifle rock-steady and take out a target hundreds of yards away while he was taking enemy fire—shook.

His vaunted control vanished like smoke on the wind.

He took her mouth, and she opened for him, meeting him eagerly as his free hand swept down her silky, delicately curved body into the narrow triangle of curls between her legs.

She was as soft there as she was everywhere else. Cupping that warm, feminine mound, he thrust his tongue into the honeyed sweetness of her mouth at the same time that he parted her satiny folds. Settling the broad tip of his finger on the wet nub at the seat of her desire, he stroked.

She made a keening sound and he echoed it with a low guttural one of his own. Yet somehow he managed to keep his touch light as he stroked again and she bucked, straining against him.

The blood was racing through his veins like a river at flood tide. Sliding his arm beneath her, careful to keep the handcuff away from her satiny skin, he snugged her torso against his own, relishing the feeling of her tightly budded nipples pressed against him. The position gave him greater freedom to move and he put it to good use, rubbing her now with a tight little circular motion. When she moaned, then moaned again, he slid his middle finger deep into her clutching, quivering heat.

She tore her mouth free of his. "Oh! No. No! I can't. I—oh!" She gulped a desperate draught of air as her head fell back and her body exploded, her tight inner muscles clamping around him.

All that slick, snug heat milking his finger demolished his restraint.

Breathing as though he'd just run ten miles uphill flat-out, he centered her beneath him and settled his hips between her thighs. Then he rocked up on one arm, guided himself into place against her and pushed.

Genevieve couldn't contain a slight cry at the squeezing fullness of that first broad inch. She was

small; he absolutely wasn't. Still she felt far more pleasure than discomfort, far more excitement than appre-
hension at his possession.

She hadn't lied. She wanted him. She just hadn't
known, hadn't ever envisioned, that sex could be like
this. That she could want, no, need, to have a man—to
have John—buried deep inside her and find that she
wanted even more.

She felt him hesitate and wrapped her legs around
him, locking him in place. "Don't stop. Don't. Stop."
Though it took all of her strength with his weight resting against her, she rocked her pelvis, propelling him
forward.

That slight movement shoved him over the edge.

With a rumble of sound that seemed to be torn from
somewhere deep inside him, he gave up the fight and
drove deep until he was socketed to the hilt inside her
tight, quivering depths.

Genevieve forgot to breathe as he withdrew, then
pushed into her again, and her body stretched to accommodate his rigid length. Despite the enormous pressure,
the promise of pleasure shimmered on the horizon in a
golden haze that danced just beyond reach as he settled
into a steadily escalating rhythm.

She arched against him, cradling him with her arms
and legs, and felt the tension ridging his big body. She
felt the sweat sheening his shoulders and the flex and
bunch of muscle in his broad back as he abruptly shifted
forward, balancing his weight on the arm sporting the
handcuff. He slipped his other forearm under her hips,
lifting her up and deepening the angle of penetration
even more.

She cried his name as his pubic bone bumped against her, stunned to find she had a frantic craving to be touched just there, like that, with exactly that grinding pressure. Gripping his hair with shaking hands, she kissed him, long, hard, wanting everything he was, everything he had to give.

They strained together, hips pumping, hearts pounding, bodies slick. Her heels drummed the back of his thighs as he rocked her higher and higher, hammering into her. She heard a distant, muffled sound and vaguely realized it was him. That he was saying her name, over and over.

The orgasm slammed into her, an eruption of pleasure that started small, deep where they were joined, and radiated outward, robbing her of breath, blanking her mind, sending out wave after wave of melting sensation, making her body quake.

She felt John thrust harder, faster, felt him above her, around her, buried deep inside her, and then he was driving toward his own satisfaction, his hips pistoning like a pile driver. She heard him cry out, felt him shudder and jerk and instinctively she bore down, stunned as she was slammed with another rush of pleasure.

He collapsed against her, crushing her into the bed. Clinging to him, she sobbed for breath, trusting him as she'd never trusted anyone else in her life to be her anchor and keep her safe.

Six

"I'm sorry." Scrubbing at the tears streaking her face, Genevieve swallowed audibly as she slowly opened her eyes. "I don't know what's wrong with me."

Lips compressed, Taggart stared down at her, careful to keep his expression blank. Outside, the weather had deteriorated. Wind buffeted the cabin, making the timbers sigh and creak, while sleet clicked against the window panes like a legion of skeletal fingertips.

It had nothing on the turbulence swirling inside him.

The waterworks had started just minutes after their mutual, mind-blowing climax. Oh, Genevieve had done her best to hide it, not making a sound except for an occasional shuddery breath.

But twined together the way they were like two strands of the same rope, there'd been no way to miss the way her shoulders shook. No way to overlook the warm slide of her tears on his skin as she clung to him, her face buried in the crook of his neck.

It cut. Unexpectedly deep. Clearly, he'd hurt her. Which shouldn't be such a big surprise given that she was half his weight and stood no taller than his shoulder. Yet that hadn't stopped him there at the end from totally losing control.

No, not *losing* it, damn it. That somehow implied his actions had been unintentional. There'd been nothing the least accidental about the way he'd kicked his control to the curb and stomped it to paste because he'd been in a fever to bury himself deep inside of her.

And Genevieve—who'd nearly stopped his heart with the inexplicable gift of herself—had paid the price. She'd been so small and tender and tight and he'd been too big, too impatient, too rough.

Oh, yeah, he thought grimly. His fault. Proof once again that he wasn't a man to trust.

Although, when he stopped to consider, part of him was of the opinion that, given the reason they were there together in the first place, she damn well should have figured that out for herself.

Yeah, well—if she didn't get it before, she does now.

Yet guilt still pricked at him. Frustrated—with himself, with the entire situation—he peeled her hands from his neck, shifted the damn chain out of his way and eased onto his back, putting some much needed distance between them. "I'm the one who should apologize," he said stiffly. "I never should've touched you."

"What?" Her response was punctuated by a watery little hiccup.

"I hurt you." He stared sightlessly into the dark. "I'm sorry."

"No. *No.*" He froze, caught completely off guard as she swiped one more time at her eyes, then twisted onto her side, propped herself on her elbow and scooted right back up against him. "You didn't hurt me. Absolutely not."

"Yeah, right."

"No, really—"

"Uh-huh. You always cry after sex," he said caustically, doing his best to ignore his body's brazen response to the warm curves plastered against him. "There's just something about coming that makes you feel all weepy and sentimental—"

"I never had an orgasm before."

The quiet statement shocked him into silence. Forgetting himself, he turned his head to stare at her and felt something deep inside him flinch as he saw the tears still clinging to the sweep of her eyelashes.

He was damned if he knew what to say.

Another blast of wind shook the cabin. In the time it took before it darted away, twin apples of color had stained her cheeks. Averting her eyes, she gave a weary little sigh, then surprised him all over again by settling trustingly against him, resting her cheek on his shoulder. "I thought…I couldn't. That there was something wrong with me. And then tonight, with you, everything changed. I guess it just got to me."

Totally at a loss, he cradled his arm around her, not knowing what else to do.

"I'm sorry," she went on. "I didn't mean to worry you."

She didn't mean to worry him. God. How was he supposed to respond to *that?*

Well, that was easy. *Don't say anything, dumbass. Do the woman a favor and blow her off. Tell her you were glad to be of service, but now that the fun and games are over it's time to get back to reality.*

And the reality was, he wasn't her friend and God knew he'd rather have burning splinters shoved under his fingernails than be her confidant. So the best, the only thing to do, was tell her to get the hell away from him while he was still in such a benevolent mood.

"Trust me, there's absolutely nothing wrong with you, sweetheart. Except that the guys in your past were incompetent morons." *Sweetheart?* Holy mother of mercy. Where had that come from? And why should the idea of somebody else touching her all of a sudden make his jaw tight?

"Maybe," she said uncertainly.

"No maybe about it."

"Unless—"

"What?"

"Maybe it's just…you." She was silent a moment, as if considering her own words. Then she raised her head and pressed her lips to the underside of his jaw. "Thanks," she said softly.

Alarm rumbled through him. It seemed no matter what he did or said, he just kept making things worse. If he didn't shut up *now,* she might actually get some twisted idea that he was worth caring about or something.

And if she knew the first thing about him, she'd realize that nothing could be further from the truth. "Forget it," he said brusquely. "Just…try to get some sleep, okay?"

She pushed up on her elbow and stared down at him. "But—"

"Look, this isn't open for discussion. You're sleeping right here, with me, tonight. The sound of your teeth chattering earlier annoyed the crap out of me, and I'm not about to give you another chance to poke me with that damn broom. So just shut up, close your eyes and let's call it a night." Tightening his arm around her, strictly to underscore his words, he pulled her back down to his side, ignoring the aches and pains in his bruised muscles that were once again making themselves known. "There's not much time left before daylight gets here anyway."

Wisely, she kept her mouth shut and resettled her head on his shoulder. They lapsed into a silence which, if not exactly companionable, was still a hell of an improvement over the sound of him babbling things he was sure to regret in the morning.

Taking a firm grip on the excess of emotion roiling around inside him, he did his best to relax. He doubted he'd sleep, but he could at least try to rest.

"John?"

"What?"

"Do you think we could pull the covers up? I'm starting to get a little chilled."

She wasn't just starting, he realized, as he felt her shiver and realized her skin had grown cool to the touch. Feeling grim all over again, he shifted her away from him, rolled onto his side, then pulled her back into the cradle of his body and yanked the covers up to her chin.

"Better?" he said gruffly.

She spooned her round little butt into his lap and rested her silky back against his chest. "Yes."

That made one of them happy, he thought, inhaling the faintly flowery scent of her hair. Swallowing a sigh, he snugged an arm around her waist to anchor her in place and propped his cheek on his tethered arm.

"John?"

"*What?*"

"Just…thanks."

Oh, yeah, no doubt about it. When his time came, he was going straight to hell. "Get some sleep, Genevieve."

God knew, he wasn't going to.

Wrapped in the delicious heat of Taggart's arms, Genevieve drifted in a dream world between waning sleep and dawning consciousness.

Then the source of all that scrumptious warmth shifted, bumping the part of himself that was exclusively male against her thigh and she was catapulted into full awareness.

Her stomach jumped. No way had she dreamt *that* up.

Cautiously, she opened her eyes, greeted by a flood of gray-white morning light. To her bemusement, she realized the satiny cushion under her cheek really was the bulge of muscle padding the underside of Taggart's arm. And that the muscle-ridged expanse of bronze rising and falling inches from her face was his chest and not that of a Michelangelo statue come to life.

Warily shifting her gaze downward, she saw that their legs were indeed tangled together.

Unable to help herself, she studied him *there,* taking a good long look at the masculine anatomy framed by a cloud of jet-black hair. Its shape was exotically different from her own. Even in sleep it looked substantial, and, as she now had good reason to know, Taggart certainly knew just what to do with—

Heat slapped her cheeks. She squeezed her eyes shut, but there was no retreat as the ribald thought tripped a floodgate in her mind, spilling memories into it of the previous night.

She saw herself clinging to Taggart like a vine to a trellis. She recalled her explosive response to the greedy pull of his mouth on her nipples. She remembered explicitly what it felt like to have those big, hard hands on her and those long, clever fingers inside her. And even if she lived to be ninety, she'd never forget the incredible sense of being irrevocably claimed that had come as he'd pushed himself into her, making them one.

A tangle of need, desire and longing reignited inside her, making her heart thump in the back of her throat. It was hard to believe that a mere twenty-four hours ago she hadn't known such feelings existed, much less made the acquaintance of the man who'd inspired them. It was equally difficult to accept how quickly she'd come to crave both Taggart and the pleasures he'd taught her.

Yet most illogical by far was her realization that, for the first time since she'd walked into her home and found Seth with a gun in his hand, standing over his best friend's lifeless body, she actually felt safe.

That wasn't merely foolish; it was dangerous. She might have been forever changed by last night's events, but her situation remained the same. She didn't think for a minute that Taggart was going to wake up this morning, announce he was quitting his job and demand she run away with him to Tahiti.

No, whatever destination she settled on in the next few hours, she'd be making the trip alone.

Still, one way or another, she *was* leaving. Just as soon as she could put together some food for him and collect her things.

She staunchly ignored the unexpected squeeze of her heart, assuring herself its only cause was the thought of all the stunning sexual fulfillment she'd never experience now.

It had nothing to do with the idea of cutting herself off from the man who'd provided it. After all, there was always a chance she'd eventually find someone else with whom she would share such electric, stomach-hollowing chemistry.

Even if based on her past history she highly doubted it.

Even if before this her sexual experiences had never even come close to what they'd shared last night.

Even if she felt repelled by the mere thought of being with anyone but John.

She shook off her misgivings, reminding herself that the only thing that was one-hundred-percent certain was she couldn't stay here. Because if it was hard to leave him after just one night, what would it be like after two, three or four? If she felt this sort of connection to him in the wake of a few hours spent sharing the sheets, how would it feel to get acquainted to the point where they actually made love?

It didn't bear thinking about it.

So she wouldn't. *That* at least—refusing to dwell on what was beyond her reach and getting on with her life because she had no other choice—was something with which she had experience.

She forced open her eyes, then blinked as she saw with more than a little fascination that the part of Taggart that had initially inspired her soul-searching was now more impressive than it had been before.

Her pulse quickened. Easing her head back, she shifted her focus to his face—and found herself staring straight into his limpid, jade-colored eyes. To her surprised relief, they were still clouded with sleep.

She took the opportunity to study their owner. Without his usual guarded expression, he looked younger, she decided. Younger, more approachable—but not a jot less masculine. From his rumpled hair to the beard shadowing his cheeks to the hard play of muscle that flexed with his every breath, he was the embodiment of all things male. Just looking at him made her feel quivery inside. "Hey," she said softly.

His heavy-lidded gaze flicked from her eyes to her mouth, lingered for the space of a heartbeat, then came back up. "Hey yourself."

His voice was morning-husky and tickled deliciously along her nerve endings. With a little jolt, she realized she no longer felt any fear when she looked at him. Oh, he was still a formidable opponent, and the knowledge that he was the one who'd be after her in the near future was scary without a doubt.

But when it came to the man himself... He'd more than watched out for her in the past hours, displaying a gruff gentleness, a near-tenderness, that was a direct contradiction to his tough outer shell.

Even though she knew she shouldn't, she surrendered to temptation. She leaned forward and pressed her mouth to his hot skin, slowly stringing kisses from his collarbone to feast on the pulse of his smooth, strong throat.

His skin smelled faintly musky and made her senses swim. By the time she finally lifted her head, she realized with a mixture of amusement and despair that her hands were shaking.

Good job, Genevieve. Why don't you make this even harder by torturing yourself with fresh reminders of what you're about to walk away from?

She blew out a breath, trying to resurrect her composure, then blew it out again in a little gasp as Taggart cupped the back of her head. "John—"

In one fluid movement he slid lower and silenced her by closing his mouth over hers.

She told herself it was just a kiss. Men and women all over the world kissed every day. Lips met and clung. Teeth nipped plump flesh, mouths parted, tongues tangled lazily, then thrust and retreated, kindling inner fires and evoking images of another type of invasion....

Her body flushed as want became need, making her ache for his possession. She tore her mouth away from his. "*No.* Don't. We can't."

He jerked back. "What's the matter?"

Her heart stuttered and her courage faltered as she saw the very real concern on his face. In that moment she wanted nothing more than to turn back the clock, resume their embrace, follow it to its natural conclusion. "I... That is—" She swallowed. "How's your head?" What on earth was she doing? Could she possibly make a worse hash of this?

He now appeared not simply wide awake, but unmistakably wary, as well. "It's okay."

"Good. That's good."

"It is, huh?" His eyes narrowed and every vestige of warmth slowly drained from his face. "Maybe you better tell me what's going on."

Clutching the sheet to her breasts like a shield, she shifted away from him and sat up, hating that she was about to end their fragile truce and make him angry.

She forced herself to meet his gaze squarely anyway. "Under the circumstances, it wouldn't be right for me—for us— I just can't take advantage of you this way. It wouldn't be fair."

His eyebrows winged up and something—disbelief, dismay?—flashed across his face, then was gone behind that controlled facade. He sat up, dragging the chain with him, and for a second his attention fixed on something beyond her before once more settling over her like an enfolding cloak.

He propped himself against the headboard and considered her, seemingly unaffected by both the cold and his own nudity. "Define circumstances," he said finally, after what felt like an eternity.

"Well...you're my prisoner." She made no attempt to evade him as he reached out with his free hand and skimmed his fingers down her arm. "You need to know, you have the right to know—" surely her next words would set him off "—that since you're so clearly okay, I plan to leave. Today." *While I still can.*

"Huh." Measuring his words, he slowly stroked his thumb over the pulse now pounding in her wrist. "And that's why we're sitting here talking instead of—"

"*Yes*." Perplexed and more than a little unnerved by his reaction—or lack of one—she fought to keep her voice steady. "I'm leaving, John. And nothing you say or do is going to stop me." She flicked her gaze to the warm weight of his hand, then back to his face and lifted her chin. "I mean, obviously you can delay me for a while but you can't keep me by your side indefinitely. Sooner or later you're going to get hungry or sleepy or have to answer the call of nature and that'll be the end of it."

"You think so?"

"I know so. I wish—" She started to say she wished she could stay, then caught herself. Not only wasn't it strictly true, but it wouldn't change anything and he probably wouldn't believe her anyway. "Well, never mind that. No matter what I wish, I have to do what's best for Seth."

"And you actually believe defying the court, taking the law into your own hands, is it?"

"Yes. No." She raked a hand through her hair. "I don't know. But until something changes or I come up with a better solution, it's all I have."

Again, for a moment that stretched interminably, he simply stared at her. Finally, he gave a slight shrug. "Yeah, well, then I don't imagine you're going to like what I'm about to say. Because you're not going anywhere, Genevieve. Not today. Probably not tomorrow. Maybe not even the day after that."

Her stomach hollowed. Not certain if it was because

he was finally being unreasonable after she'd done her best to be honest—or the deplorable flutter of excitement she felt at the idea of being trapped in bed with him a little while longer—she did her best to ignore it. "Who's going to stop me, John? You?"

Again he glanced toward the far side the room, then deliberately released his hold on her and folded his arms behind his neck, ignoring the heavy chain as if it weighed nothing. "Nope." He inclined his head. "That."

Exasperated, she twisted around—and felt her stomach plummet.

Because beyond the windows, the world had been transformed into a sea of white. Snow fell in swirling, relentless sheets that choked the air, reducing visibility to zero as it blanketed everything in sight.

And try as she might, Genevieve couldn't see a single sign that it might let up anytime soon.

Seven

"So how come this place doesn't have a woodstove?"

Seated at the kitchen table, Genevieve gave a start of surprise. Except for a few unavoidable utterances of "yes," "no" and "thanks," it was the first time Taggart had spoken to her since she'd climbed out of bed, dragged on her sleep shirt and trudged to the windows to stare forlornly out at the snow more than nine hours ago.

In the interim, they'd both washed and dressed, shared a trio of meals and not much else.

Deliberately rattling the chain that still tethered him, he'd made the bed, brooded, exercised, stared at the ceiling, paced, brooded some more.

She'd reorganized the kitchen, hauled firewood, read an entire mystery cover to cover, hauled more wood and wondered how long it would be before the power, which had begun to flicker at midmorning, went out for good.

She'd gotten the answer an hour after dusk, she thought, glancing at the oil lamp providing her with light, one of three currently staving off the darkness. At least they had plenty of kerosene, a generous supply of food and enough heat from the fireplace to keep them alive, if not exactly toasty.

"There used to be a stove," she told him. "When my uncle was alive." Frowning in concentration at the piece of paper before her, she tucked one side of the blanket covering her legs a little tighter.

"So what happened?"

She felt the weight of his gaze like a touch. Reluctantly, she stilled her pen and glanced over at him.

And wished instantly she hadn't.

Half an hour earlier he'd embarked on his second exercise routine of the day, doing several hundred each of sit-ups, push-ups, ab crunches and the like at a bruising pace. One that would have put her in the hospital for sure, but had left him barely winded.

Now he sat sprawled on the floor, stripped down to his jeans, back propped against the bed, one long leg cocked. The ends of his cropped, inky hair were damp from exertion, the perfect frame for his compelling face with its straight nose, strong cheekbones and hard mouth. Sweat sheened his shoulders as well, gleamed on the hard planes of his chest and the sinewy ripples of his abdomen, while the lamplight tinted his skin to toasted gold.

Need punched low and deep, making her breath

catch and squeeze in her lungs. Appalled, annoyed, she sat up a little straighter in the chair. What was it about him that stripped away her usual defenses? What dark magic did he possess that made her burn to scrub her palms against the muscle bulging in his arms, to rub her cheek against his chest, to sample the salt on his skin with her tongue?

She didn't have a clue, so she jerked her gaze away, returning it to the papers spread out on the tabletop.

"After my uncle died—" *come on, come on, get a grip* "—this place became a summer vacation rental. Apparently fireplaces are sexy and woodstoves aren't, and the agency that manages things didn't feel there was room for both. Luckily they allowed for a heat insert along with the glass doors; otherwise we'd be freezing our fannies off for sure."

"Huh."

She held her breath. When he didn't say anything more, she relaxed just a fraction and picked up her pen, hoping he couldn't see the tremor shaking her fingers, praying he'd leave her in peace.

"What are you writing, anyway?"

Darn it. For a man who hadn't shown an inclination toward conversation for most of time that she'd known him, he was certainly chatty all of a sudden. Maybe if she pretended to be too absorbed to hear him—

"A book? Your memoirs? *Genevieve's Life on the Run?*"

Her mouth tightened. "A letter."

"To your brother?"

"No. A detective agency. In Denver."

"Why?"

"Because eventually somebody is actually going to listen to me and take a hard look at Seth's case."

He was silent just long enough for her to start to hope he'd taken the hint. And then—

"So you're…what? Contacting private investigators, asking them to take up your case?" His voice held a hint of incredulity he made no attempt to camouflage.

It was like a sharp jab at a raw wound. Her head came up. "I'm writing everybody. I have been for months. Police. Politicians. Attorneys. I'd write Oprah herself if I thought she could help."

"Is that what you meant this morning about waiting for something to change before you'll consider turning yourself in?"

She nodded. Although she didn't recall saying the words, she'd said a number of things earlier that day she hadn't exactly planned. "Yes. I suppose it is."

He pursed his lips. "And if someone does take that hard look?"

"Then they'll have to at least consider what I already know. That Seth's telling the truth. He isn't the one who killed Jimmy."

He started to shake his head. "Damn it, Genevieve—"

"Don't," she said sharply, coming to her feet. She was tired, cold and off balance from what they'd shared. Not to mention overwhelmed by her own unfamiliar emotions, and in no mood to be lectured, particularly by him. "You don't know anything about it."

He surged upright as well. "I know enough to be damn skeptical about your brother's version of events. He had means, motive and opportunity, and there's nothing in the police report to support his claim that he saw a stranger fleeing the scene. Which, just so we're clear, is a really lame defense, as anybody who's ever seen *The Fugitive* knows."

Ignoring the gibe, she stared at him in surprise. "You read the police report?"

"I do my homework. When it comes to finding people, Steele Security has a firm policy about not taking on ambiguous cases. We do the best we can to make sure we're not tracking down innocents and returning them to the bad guys."

"If you read the police report," she persisted, kicking the blanket out of her way as she came around the table to meet him face-to-face, "you know the gun was Jimmy's, not Seth's."

"So? Your brother knew where it was kept, had easy access and out of the three people at the scene—you, him and the victim—he was the only one with powder residue on his hands."

"That's because he took a shot at the real killer—"

"Yeah, right. Come on, Genevieve, you're smarter than that. Forget the one-armed man and focus on the gun. For your brother's version of events to work, James Dunn would've had to bring it with him to your house and conveniently surprise an intruder who felt compelled to confront him, wrest away the gun and shoot to kill. It makes no sense. There's no gain, no motive and absolutely no evidence—not a hair, not a single fingerprint—to support it.

"Seth, on the other hand, had a damn good reason for what he did. The money from Dunn's life insurance was just enough to save his precious ski shop. But he had to move fast since Dunn had come back from vacation with the news he'd met someone and they were getting married. Soon. At which time he no doubt intended to change his will and everything else, making his new wife his beneficiary."

"Are you finished?"

"Yeah, pretty much."

Words crowded her mouth, clamoring to be given a voice. She had at least a dozen things she wanted to say, a dozen facts she wanted to share, a dozen arguments she could make as to why he was wrong.

Yet staring at him, taking in the stubborn set of his jaw, she realized she didn't think she could stand it if he refused to listen. The only thing that would be worse was if he did agree to hear her out and then, like everyone else, flatly rejected the possibility that Seth might be innocent.

It would be a major blow. More, she thought, than she could handle.

She tried to tell herself she was being dramatic. That it was her exhaustion speaking, that she was having some sort of unprecedented overreaction to the events of the past forty-eight hours.

Yet she still couldn't risk it. At this moment in time, defying logic, defeating common sense, he mattered to her, and that was all there was to it.

"Well that makes two of us." Coming to a sudden decision, she turned on her heel, marched into the kitchen and blew out the lantern glowing on the counter. Swiveling, she backtracked to the table, jammed her nearly finished letter into the correspondence folder and snatched up the blanket.

"What the hell are you doing?"

"Going to bed."

"Now? We're not done—"

"I am. It's been a long day and I'm tired. I don't want to deal with this—" *with you* "—now." Her movements stiff with suppressed emotion, she leaned forward to snuff out the second lamp.

"Just leave it, all right?" Taggart said sharply.

Surprised at the vehemence in his voice, she jerked away. "Sure. Whatever." Unable to help herself, she turned to look at him, but his expression was closed, his gaze shuttered.

And just like that, the memory of how safe she'd felt in his arms the previous night came rushing back. Before she could get a grip, her lips trembled.

His mouth tightened. "Damn it, Genevieve—"

"Let it go, John. Please." Walking to the couch, she quickly peeled off her jeans and one of the two sweaters she had on over a thermal shirt. Then she extinguished the lantern on the end table, climbed into her sleeping bag and dragged it and the blanket up to her ears. "Just…let it go."

Closing her eyes, she curled up and prayed for the oblivion of sleep.

Taggart stared at the shadows cast by the glow of the lamplight as they danced gently on the ceiling above his head.

Outside, the wind still surged and gusted, but it had settled down from a constant howl to a whispered growl. Inside there was only silence, except for the occasional crackle of the fire and the soft ebb and flow of Genevieve's breathing.

Taggart's mind, however, was anything but quiet.

Thoughts clashed and emotions rumbled, twisting, tangling and battling for recognition as he tried to sort out what it was he was feeling. Yet when he boiled everything down to the basic facts, he found himself pretty much where he'd been for most of the day.

Genevieve found him sexually appealing. That he at least understood, since he felt the same for her.

It was the rest of it that kept hanging him up.

She believed he had "rights" that obliged her to be honest. She worried about being fair to him. She'd even insisted on forgoing pleasure because—he blew out a pent-up breath—she didn't want to take advantage of him.

And what had he given her in return? Great sex. Zero companionship. One minute of conversation and a brutal recap of all the reasons why she should doubt herself and abandon her brother.

Man, was he a prince or what?

He scrubbed his hands over his face and tried to wrestle things back into perspective. It wasn't as if he'd deliberately set out to be the world's biggest bastard, he reminded himself. Last night, at least when he'd first yanked her into bed, it had been with a vague but genuine desire to save her from potential harm.

He sure as hell hadn't planned what had happened next. But then, there'd been no way he could have foreseen such a simple contact sparking a blaze that would consume them both. And in his own defense, in what had probably been the only time in his life he'd actually deserved a medal, when it had seemed that she wanted him to stop, he had.

She'd been the one who'd thrown gasoline on the fire and caution to the wind.

She'd also made the first move this morning. It had been her mouth branding a trail up his chest, her lips nuzzling his throat, her soft little body lighting him up as she snuggled close. And yeah, presented with such an unmistakable invitation, he'd kissed her back and been fully prepared to do even more, but really—who could blame him?

He was a man, not some pious saint, and he'd spent half the night with her all over him like jam slathered on toast. Yet for the second time in less than a dozen hours, when she'd called a halt, he'd stopped.

If he had it to do over again, knowing what he did now, he'd be damn tempted to just kiss her senseless, bury himself as deep as he could get in her sweet, squeezing heat, and skip the whole incredible, mystifying, logic-defying conversation that had followed.

Because, sweet holy mother of God, just how the hell *was* he supposed to respond to a woman who, instead of taking a strip off him for taking advantage of her and then doing everything she could to keep him at arm's length, seemed dead set on looking out for him?

Well, here's an idea: Ignore her most of a day, then get right in her face and demand she admit her brother's a stone-cold murderer.

Okay, so maybe that hadn't been the best way to go. Although, according to every shred of evidence he'd seen, it was a slam dunk that Seth Bowen had killed his friend Jimmy Dunn.

Only Genevieve didn't think so. But then, that was hardly a surprise. If she'd give him, someone she'd known for a mere handful of days, the benefit of the doubt, then it was to be expected that she'd fight with her last breath for her brother. God knew, he'd do the same for any of his.

And yet… Would he give up his home, his livelihood, his reputation, his freedom, based on nothing more than blind devotion?

He didn't think so.

And from what he knew of Genevieve—smart, resourceful, overly responsible Genevieve, who had a moral code strong enough to dictate she stay and care for a wounded enemy rather than exploit another's misfortune and make tracks while she could—neither would she.

And that meant…what, exactly? He blew out a breath. Damned if he knew. Which, he supposed, went a long way toward explaining why he felt all tied up inside.

The swishing sound of nylon rubbing against itself whispered through the darkness. Gratefully, he pounced on the distraction, drawing back deeper into the shadows as one of the couch springs gave a groan and Genevieve unexpectedly sat up.

Smothering a yawn, she stood. After a quick glance in his direction, she crossed to the hearth, added a piece of wood to the fire, shut the glass doors and straightened.

Turning, she looked briefly toward the ladder leading to the loft, then glanced his way again. Appearing to reach a decision, she scrubbed her hands up her arms as she tiptoed across the room, past the bed and disappeared into the bathroom.

Well, hell. Now what?

Even as asked the question, he knew. Just as he knew that for once in his life he wasn't going to think it to death, weigh every last pro and con, try to calculate everything that could go wrong.

She had, after all, left a light on for him.

He was on his feet and waiting for her, his decision made, his resolve firmly in place, when she opened the door.

"Oh!" With a stutter of surprise, she took a half step back and clapped a hand to her heart. "God, John, you scared me. What are you doing up?" She sidled to her left, clearly intending to brush past him.

He mirrored her movement, blocking her path. "Get in the bed, Genevieve."

She jerked to a stop, her gaze flying to his face. "What?"

"You can be as mad at me as you want, but that's no reason to be stupid. It's cold and we've got a limited amount of firewood. It makes sense to share our body heat."

"Sense?" She took another sideways step. "I don't think—"

"Good." Again, he planted himself in her path. "Go with that."

Her head tipped back and her eyes narrowed. "Get out of my way."

"No."

She conferred a long, searching look on him, her gaze for once impossible to read.

He gave a faint sigh. "I'm not going to jump you, if that's what's worrying you."

At that, she lowered her head, ensuring he had no chance of getting so much as a glimpse of her expression. "I never gave it a thought," she said coolly.

His kitten had claws. Not sure whether to be annoyed or amused, he reached out, cupped her shoulder, nudged her toward the bed. "Go on then. Get in."

Her chin came up stubbornly, but the effect was ruined as she shivered, this time more violently than before. "Oh, all right. If you insist."

Shrugging away his hand, she stepped over the trailing chain, walked the few paces to the bed, ignoring him as he backed out of her way, continuing to bar her escape. She tossed back the covers, slid between the sheets and turned away, her face to the wall.

His mission accomplished, he peeled off his jeans and crawled in beside her. For half a second, he considered honoring the not-so-subtle request implicit in her ironing-board posture that he leave her the hell alone.

But nobody had ever accused him of being a sensitive, New Age kind of guy. With a ruthless directness that felt good after too many hours spent foundering in the quicksand of his emotions, he slung his arm around her and crowded close.

Her bare legs and the exposed curves of her butt were icy cold. Rather than recoil, he threw his leg over hers, sharing what warmth he could.

He did hesitate, however, if only for an instant, before he smoothed the thick, soft ends of her hair away from her nape, bent his head and settled his mouth there.

After all, the issue of where he'd be spending eternity was a done deal. And the part of him pressing against the curve of her firm little bottom was already as hard as an iron rod. But what decided the issue was the taste of her on his tongue, like sunlight and sweetness and the promise of summer to a man who'd lived with his soul's winter bleakness far too long.

Still, he had every intention of going slowly, of testing the waters, of backing off at the first sign of resistance.

But even before he began the slow slide of his parted lips toward her ear, she was twisting around, anchoring her fingers in his hair, deciding their fate with the soft cry of his name.

"John. Oh, yes." She pressed even closer at the same time as she arched her neck to provide him even greater access. "Yes."

Not gasoline on the fire this time, he thought, as desire scorched him. Rocket fuel.

Her back bowed as she strained toward him. It seemed the most natural thing in the world to slip his fingers beneath the layers of shirts she had on, slide his hand up the satin tautness of her stomach, over the sturdy bump of her ribs and under the band of her bra.

Both of them groaned as he rubbed his palm over the exquisite softness of her stiff little nipple.

Then they groaned again as she reached for him, skimming her hand under his waistband to close around his turgid length.

"Easy," he choked out. "We've got the whole night—"

"No." She measured him with a stroke of her palm that had him clenching his teeth. "*Now.* Now, now, *now.*"

Not rocket fuel, either. Nitroglycerine, explosive and volatile.

Breathing hard, arms and hands colliding, they hurried to strip away each other's clothing. He was easy; his briefs took a single slide and jerk. Genevieve's panties and various tops took longer, and he swore under his breath as he rapped himself in the elbow with the chain as he grappled with the clasp of her bra. Finally winning the battle, he tossed the flimsy undergarment away.

Before the strip of nylon and lace could hit the floor, she was straddling him, her silky thighs gripping his hips, her fingers digging into his straining biceps, her teeth grazing his throat. "Hurry, John. Hurry up."

Her urgency filled some deep, profound hunger he hadn't known he possessed. He wanted her, only her, in a way he'd never wanted anything or anyone else.

He felt her hands tremble as she cupped his face and then her lips were on his. The kick from that simple contact reverberated in every nerve and fiber of his being as her sweetness filled him, washed him clean, sustained him.

He slicked his hands the length of her back, down the satiny skin that covered the delicate curves of rib and spine, the bend of her waist, the swell of her hips.

She quivered beneath his touch. She rocked her pelvis with more instinct than finesse, rubbing herself against him, and the suggestion of what was to come made his vision dim. Bringing his hand around, he gently slicked the pad of his thumb along the valley of her sex.

She was wet, ready for him, and he—who'd always prided himself on his restraint—had none.

He needed this joining, needed her display of trust, needed *her.*

Needed. And took.

With a flex of his hips he positioned himself and thrust, sliding deep inside her.

He felt her clench around him, and wasn't sure which of them was more shocked as the first wave of pleasure ripped through her. Unprepared for her hair-trigger response, he still managed to catch her startled cry with his mouth.

Cupping the warm swell of her breasts in his palms, he squeezed her distended nipples with slowly increasing pressure and fought the urge to ravish her. Instead, although the effort had sweat beading across his nose, he forced himself to keep still, to let her ride the crest, ride him. Hearing her call his name, feeling her drive herself over the edge, holding her as she took the long, shattering fall to completion, he couldn't imagine how she'd ever thought herself passionless.

It seemed an eternity before she finally lay spent, her shuddering breath fanning his throat, her fingers slack on his shoulders.

"Genevieve." His voice was thick.

"Hmm?"

He pressed a kiss to her temple, smoothed a shaking hand over her hair. "Can you sit up?"

She didn't reply for a second, then slowly raised her head. "What?"

"I want to see you." Catching her by the shoulders, he pushed her upright, swallowing hard as he got his first good look at her face.

Her lips were passion-swollen, her cheeks flushed,

her hair tousled. But it was her eyes, heavy-lidded, opaque with pleasure and dark with wonder as she gazed down at him, that set the muscle ticking in his jaw.

He wasn't some callow kid. And though he didn't claim to understand it, there was a certain kind of woman who'd always seemed to find his very indifference a challenge, so he'd never lacked for sexual partners.

As he'd admitted to himself earlier, lust he understood. But this... He'd never looked at a woman and felt this kind of gut-twisting tenderness, much less this confounding compulsion to brand her as his own.

He felt his heart pounding, even before she reached down and touched her fingers to his mouth. "It's all right, John. It's all right."

He told himself there was no way she could know what he was feeling. Told himself, but didn't believe it. There was a connection between them, a bond, and for this moment in time, he was done fighting it. "Take me. Take all of me."

"Yes. Oh, yes."

Gripping her waist, he lifted her up until they teetered on the edge of separation, then brought her sliding down, his breath hissing out at the squeezing tightness.

Yet as good as it was, it wasn't enough. He needed more. He needed everything.

In a single, powerful movement he caught her to him and reversed their positions, keeping himself buried deep inside her even as he shoved the excess chain out of their way. Bringing his mouth down on hers, he kissed her with barely contained violence as he began to move.

He couldn't get close enough. Deep enough. Muscles straining, he drove forward and felt something inside him give way as she didn't simply welcome him, but rose up, met him stroke for stroke, and begged for more.

He lost it then, going wild, slamming against her, again and again, feeling as if the top of his head was going to blow off when the velvet glove of her body tightened and quivered once more, and she mindlessly cried his name.

The sound shivered through him, triggering a colossal landslide of his senses. His body exploded in a climax that blew him apart, turned him inside out.

Yet even as his strength deserted him and he collapsed into her cradling arms, some part of him recognized that what had just passed between them wasn't merely sex, but a mating.

Because somehow she seemed to have freed a portion of the heart that he'd walled off long ago.

Eight

Genevieve lay cradled in the curve of Taggart's arm, her head pillowed on his shoulder.

Despite the intensity of their lovemaking, she could feel the tension still thrumming through him. She wondered at its cause, but at the same time she understood him well enough to realize he was accustomed to relying on himself, on working through matters in his own time and way, and that it wouldn't be wise to push.

Besides, if he was feeling even half as unsettled as she was, his restlessness was understandable. Because something was happening between them, she thought, as she slowly stroked her fingers over the warm taut skin above his hip. Something beyond the powerful physical attraction that had them firmly in its hot-fingered grip.

And it was happening fast—too fast for comfort or easy answers. In the space of mere days they'd gone from being total strangers to sharing a connection that was as strong and elemental as the storm that had stranded them together. It was daunting and more than a little frightening, yet Genevieve could no more deny it than she could reverse the weather.

She could do something about the oppressive silence that lay over them like a smothering weight, however. "John?"

"Hmm?"

"How come you didn't tell me your last name was Steele the day we met?"

He tensed a fraction, but then to her gratification the muscle beneath her cheek noticeably relaxed. "No reason to mention it."

"Oh. So what are you saying? That you only share your name on a need-to-know basis?"

"Yeah. I guess I am."

"Good grief." She raised her head to stare at him. "What exactly is Steele Security? Some sort of secret society?"

Her faintly alarmed question pried a brief, rusty laugh out of him. "Not even close."

She waited for him to go on. When he didn't, she had to fight the urge to roll her eyes. He could give a clam lessons in being closemouthed. "Explain."

His shoulders hitched. "Not much to it. It's a family business now, a partnership with my brothers, that started when Gabe—he's the oldest—left the service. He took what he'd learned in SOCom—"

"SOCom?" She settled back against him.

"Special Operations Command. It's the part of the military that has to do with the special forces units, like Delta, SEALs, Green Berets. Gabe decided he'd take a shot at offering some specialized services to the private sector that regular law enforcement can't."

When he fell silent again, she gave his hard stomach a gentle poke. "Why not?"

"A variety of reasons. A lack of time, money, manpower. Jurisdictional restrictions. Turns out he hit a real nerve, and the work just poured in."

"But what do you do?"

"Risk assessment, security evaluations, providing short-term protection for personnel and structures, that sort of thing. Mostly it's pretty tame."

"And when it isn't?"

"It depends, but the riskier stuff tends to be case-specific—hostage recovery, protecting a high-value target, going after someone who's determined not to be found."

"Like me."

"I wouldn't exactly classify you as high risk, Genevieve." He couldn't quite keep a trace of amusement from creeping into his voice. "Frustrating, yeah, and definitely annoying. But not dangerous."

"Gee, thanks." Despite her tart reply, she wasn't able to contain a slight smile of her own as they lapsed into silence, listening to the wind as it darted in to rattle the windows before streaking away. She liked his rare flashes of understated humor, even when they were directed at her. "Just how long *have* you been chasing me?"

"A while."

This time she did roll her eyes, even though he couldn't see it. "Define a while."

He answered with obvious reluctance. "A few months."

"A few *months?*" It wasn't admirable, but she felt a certain satisfaction that she'd managed to elude him for so long without even knowing he was on her trail, and it showed in her voice.

"Yeah." He made an unmistakable sound of disgust. "You care to explain where you learned how to disappear like that?"

"Oh, come on, that's a no-brainer."

"Indulge me. Lately my brain seems to be lodged somewhere other than my head. At least the one above my shoulders."

"I own a bookstore. Hence, I learned from a book. You can learn anything if you know where to look."

"Jesus. I take it back. You *are* dangerous."

Delighted, she laughed. "Thanks."

With just the whisper of a touch, he rubbed the ball of her shoulder with his thumb. "So, you gonna complete my humiliation and finally tell me how the hell you got me inside after the accident?"

"Gosh, I don't know. I'm not sure it would be wise to give away all of my secrets—"

Without warning, he twisted effortlessly so that he was above her, her body caged by his arms. His gaze drilled into her. "Talk."

She bit her lip to prevent a smile, and then unable to help herself, reached up and cupped the side of his face, enjoying the prickle of his beard against her palm. "Isn't it obvious? I carried you."

"Uh-huh. You and what army?"

"Oh, all right. If you must know—" she did her best to sound put-out, which wasn't easy when he caught the pad of her thumb between his lips and sucked, making the breath jam in her throat "—you brought yourself in. You were only unconscious for a few minutes—"

"Long enough for you to find the key to the handcuffs and get loose," he murmured, eyes suddenly gleaming dangerously.

"—before you came around enough that I could get you to slide across the seat so I could back the truck up to the cabin. You were pretty out of it, so it took some work to keep you upright and pointed in the right direction, but the end result is that you walked in under your own power."

"And let you put my own handcuffs on me, like a lamb to the slaughter."

"Yes."

He was silent a moment. "Where'd you get the chain?"

"It was in the bed of the truck."

"Lucky for you."

"No, lucky for you," she countered matter-of-factly. "Without it you'd be on a much shorter leash."

Only inches apart, they stared at each other, the seconds slowly ticking past until, to her shock, the corners of his mouth quirked an entire eighth of an inch while the skin around his eyes crinkled a similar fraction. "Pretty damn pleased with yourself, aren't you?"

Not by the wildest reach of imagination could he be said to be smiling. Still, there was something in his look that made the heat rush into her cheeks—as well as a few other places—and set her stomach to tap-dancing. She swallowed, fighting the urge to throw her dignity to the wind and just grab him. "Yes. I suppose I am."

"Yeah, well…" He lowered his head and trailed his lips from her temple to her cheek to the edge of her mouth, watching her all the while "…maybe you deserve to be."

Pleasure made her heart thump in her chest. Then he slowly flexed his hips and sank his flesh into her welcoming wetness and her already tenuous restraint vanished like dust in the wind.

Wrapping him in her arms, she claimed his mouth and eagerly gave herself up to the melting pleasure she'd only ever known with him.

Sweet holy hell, Taggart thought, as he and Genevieve lay tangled together a full two hours later, flesh damp and lungs winded, muscles quivering and bodies spent.

He didn't know what was worse. The fact that without any apparent effort she seemed able to separate his mouth from his brain and turn him into a frigging babbling brook.

Or that he couldn't keep his hands off her.

Always before he'd viewed sex like food: just another essential one needed to get by. A man got hungry, a man ate and then he pushed back from the table and walked away. Maybe every once in a while he got an unexpected taste of dessert, but it wasn't anything he couldn't live without.

But with Genevieve… Nothing was the same. *He* wasn't the same. His desire for her felt more like the inescapable need he had to breathe than a lesser, more controllable urge.

The thought sent a shiver of uneasiness shooting down his spine. Or would have, he thought caustically, if he had a nerve left to carry it.

"John?" The cause of his alarm skimmed a fingertip over the nape of his neck.

"Hmm?"

"How many brothers do you have?"

He raised his head from where it rested against the crook of her neck. "What?"

"You said you and your brothers are partners. How many of them are there?"

He hesitated, but he couldn't see the harm in answering. As topics went, in fact, it was a hell of a lot safer than the one his mind had been zeroing in on. "There are nine of us all together."

"Nine?"

"Yeah."

"Good Lord."

"What?"

"Nothing. I just…I'm trying to imagine eight more of you and it's making me a little dizzy."

Damned if her slightly horrified admission didn't handily dislodge the last of his disquiet and leave a kind of fuzzy-edged tenderness for her that was completely unlike him in its place. "I guess we do all sort of look alike: tall, dark hair."

Telling himself the feeling would pass, that it was the consequence of great sex, nothing else, he rolled more completely onto his side. He flexed his tired muscles, before settling back down so their eyes were on a level.

Genevieve stared at him expectantly.

"What?"

"Gosh, I don't know. Maybe you could tell me a little more?"

His brows knit. "Like what?"

Something flickered across her face that was either despair or amusement or a mixture of both. "Let's see. You said Gabe's the oldest. What are you? The youngest?"

"No. That'd be Jake."

"While you are…?"

"Ten months younger than Gabe. Then comes Dominic, Cooper and Deke."

"Okay." She worried her full bottom lip. "That's six. What about the other three?"

He supposed he might as well just lay it out and be done with it. "Look, we're a military family. I told you about Gabe. I was an Army Ranger, Dom, Deke and Coop were all SEALs—get the picture? Right now there are five of us in the business, while Josh, Eli and Jordan are all currently on active duty overseas. Then there's Jake. He's in his last year of college."

She blinked, trying to take it in. "Wow. Your parents must be proud. Exhausted, but proud."

He gave a little shrug. "The old man's in Florida, retired from the army, doing his own thing the way he always has. My mom passed away a long time back, when we were all still kids."

"Oh, John, I'm sorry. How terrible. That must've been hard."

There was no doubting the genuine sympathy in her voice. Still, he was shocked to hear himself agree. "Yeah. It sucked."

She reached out, stroked his upper arm as if to try and soothe away that long-ago hurt. "I'm so sorry," she said again.

Maybe because she didn't press, he found himself wanting to tell her about it. "She was in a car accident, just a minor fender bender in a parking lot, except she wasn't wearing a seat belt and she hit the steering wheel. It was the day before my birthday, and she had things to do, so she just blew the accident off. And then…something inside her was torn and…that was it. She was standing in the kitchen, icing the cake and then she was just gone."

Genevieve remained quiet, simply touching him in an age-old gesture of comfort, but her eyes were indelibly sad for him.

"I didn't handle it very well. Gabe took care of things, the way he always does, but I got angry. Skipped school. Got into fights. Broke windows and busted up fences and didn't come home at night. Eventually I got caught boosting a car. Not even Gabe could fix that, so I got shipped off to Blackhurst, a military school. It saved me." *For all the good it did—*

"I slugged a social worker once."

"What?" Genevieve's quiet statement jerked him back from the abyss. He gave a faint snort. "Yeah, right."

"I did. It was after my grandpa died. This woman told me that Seth and I might not be able to stay together in the same foster home and I punched her."

"Jesus, Gen, what are you talking about?" Except for the information that she had no known living family except her brother, and the notation that she sometimes acted as an emergency foster mother, there hadn't been a hint, either in the file he'd been given on her or among her friends, of anything like this. "How old were you?"

"Eleven."

"Where were your folks?"

"We never knew our father—or fathers. And our mom had dumped us on Gramps a year or so earlier and disappeared for good. Responsibility—" her voice took on an unfamiliar, caustic note "—was never her thing."

"And you wound up in foster care?"

"That, and group homes. It wasn't too bad, once they realized I wouldn't tolerate our being separated. We got to spend some of our vacations with Gramps's brothers and sisters, until they were gone, too. I got emancipated at seventeen, got a job, my own place and custody of Seth and that was the end of it. When my uncle Ben died, he left me this cabin and enough money to make a down payment on the bookstore."

He didn't know what to say. But Genevieve being Genevieve, he didn't have to worry about filling the silence for too long.

"I've always thought it would be sort of nice to be part of a big family," she ventured unexpectedly. "To have other people around who know your history, who know *you*. People who care what happens to you."

The hint of wistfulness in her voice, which he doubted she even realized was there, made him want to go out, track down her long-lost loser parents and give them exactly what they deserved. Yet as he knew all too well, there was no going back, no fixing the past.

There was only the here and now. "Big families do

have some benefits," he told her. "But trust me, there are drawbacks, too."

"Like what?"

"Well…" Inexplicably determined to banish the last trace of melancholy from her eyes, he considered. "I don't think I ever slept in a room alone or made a phone call without somebody listening in until I scraped together enough money to rent a hotel room when I was eighteen.

"Nothing else is sacred, either. Food, shoes, your toothbrush—you name it and it's open season. And you can forget the whole idea of "your" clothes. In a big family, if they're clean, they're fair game. Blackhurst was the first place I didn't have to hide my damn underwear against marauders."

She chuckled. "Listen to us. If we wrote a book, we'd have to call it *Poor Pitiful Childhoods.*" The chuckle got swallowed by a yawn, but when it was over, the soft smile he was starting to crave was back on her face. "God, we're a pair."

For an instant Taggart found himself thinking she was right. Then he gave himself a sharp jerk back.

No. No way would they ever be a pair, a couple, a twosome.

Because she still didn't know the truth about him. And it would be a cold day in hell before he'd allow that to change.

Nine

Genevieve jiggled from foot to foot as she rummaged through her duffel bag, searching for the bottom half of her long johns.

She was dressed in nothing but socks, panties and bra, shivering in the room that had yet to warm from the fire she'd built up first thing after climbing out of bed. The cold, as brisk as it was, wasn't the main cause of her inability to stand still, however.

That had just strolled out of the bathroom and was standing a dozen feet away, one broad shoulder propped against the doorjamb, one jeans-clad hip cocked, both muscular arms crossed over his naked chest.

She could feel Taggart's gaze like a velvet touch, making every nerve ending in her body jump.

Rationally, she knew her reaction was beyond foolish. They'd made love a dozen different ways the previous night; there wasn't any part of her body that those big hands hadn't touched, that hard mouth hadn't tasted, those always hard-to-read green eyes hadn't seen.

She was nevertheless very much aware that their intimacies had all taken place in the soft, shadowy cocoon of darkness lit by only the gentle glow of a single lantern's light.

Now she was standing, exposed, in dawn's unforgiving glare.

Yet it wasn't mere modesty alone that was making her jittery, she conceded. No, it was that Taggart's opinion of the view he was currently taking in mattered to her. Far more than she could have imagined just days ago. Definitely more than was prudent or wise.

Swallowing, she pawed through her belongings, triumphantly closing her fingers around the object of her search just as she heard Taggart make an odd sound, one that was neither sigh nor curse but a mixture of both.

Snatching the long johns to her chest, she swiveled to face him straight on. "What?"

"Nothing," he said instantly, his voice the slightest bit hoarse. His gaze skated over her. "I just—it never occurred to me Pollyanna would have a taste for killer underwear."

She glanced down at her cherry-red bra and panties, frilly lingerie being one of her few indulgences, then back at him. She frowned. "Pollyanna?"

It took a second for her question to penetrate his fascination with the embroidered roses twined strategically across various bits of sheer, transparent fabric.

When it did, his gaze shot to her face. "Forget it," he said hastily. "You look…good."

Pleasure washed through her—until she remembered what had sent her scurrying for her clothes in the first place. She watched, her pulse tripping irregularly, as he pushed away from the wall and strode a few feet closer, the chain gripped in his hand to prevent the trailing links from rapping him in the ankles.

Conflicting desires froze her in place. Her heart urged her to cross the space that separated them, step into his arms, run her hands across the taut skin of his chest and abdomen and watch the glint in his eyes turn to fire.

Her head preached caution, warning her that for both their sakes, the best thing she could do was stay out of his reach, at least until she figured out for sure if—

"What's wrong?"

"Nothing. I—" Darned if she didn't start to take a step toward him, only to be brought up short when the warmth suddenly vanished from his face as he looked past her.

His eyes watchful, he gestured toward the fleece shirt and thermal vest she'd laid out in addition to her usual jeans, winter silks and pair of sweaters. "Looks like you're getting geared up to go someplace."

She wondered what it would take to win his trust. Or if it were even possible, given the reason they were together in the first place.

The one thing she didn't question was that it mattered—that *he* mattered—since the question of how much was precisely what was fueling her urgent need for some space. Even if it came at the cost of a potential case of frostbite.

"It occurred to me that I may have paid a few years back to replace Uncle Ben's old generator," she said. "I thought I'd make a trip to the shed to see if I'm right, and if I am, to see if I can get the thing running."

He glanced out the window, contemplating the sullen gray sky and the snow that could now be measured in feet rather than inches. Thanks to the ever-present wind, huge drifts of white, some of them taller than she was, dominated the frigid landscape.

"Forget it," he said flatly, that pale, enigmatic gaze coming back to her. "We can live without power a while longer."

Thinking that she knew what was worrying him, she dredged up a reassuring smile. "Don't worry. I'm coming back. Even I know I wouldn't get far in the truck with this much snow on the ground."

His mouth tightened, but he was silent as she pulled on her silk bottoms, long johns and then her one pair of flannel-lined jeans. "That's not the problem."

"Oh? Then what is?"

"Get real, Genevieve. It's probably ten below out there if you factor in the wind chill." He stooped down and slid his own shirts up the chain, then impatiently began the process of putting them on, dragging the black cotton knit over his head, then untwisting the arms of his big flannel shirt and shrugging into it. "If anything goes wrong, if a branch comes down or you stumble into a drift that's over your head… Hell, it's not worth taking the chance for a generator that may not exist. God knows—" his voice darkened as he gave the chain a disgusted rattle "—I won't be any help."

So he did care. At least a little. Her heart swelled,

much the way it had when she'd been perched on the edge of the bed a little while ago, mooning over him as he stood at the bathroom sink scraping the beard off his cheeks and she'd found herself thinking—

No. Don't go there. Not here in front of him.

"I'll be fine." Her own multiple layers of clothing in place, she zipped up her vest, stepped into her boots, then bent down to tie them, glad for the excuse to hide her face. "I really want to check it out. I mean, I can live without heat or lights but not hot water," she said, injecting a false cheerfulness into her voice. "And I'd rather not have to cook outside on the barbecue if I don't have to—"

"Okay, fine." His voice was brutally clipped. "If it means so damn much to you, then undo this frigging handcuff and let me take care of it. If there is a generator out there, I'll at least be able to get it to run."

Straightening, she hesitated, unexpectedly tempted to do what he asked. To go ahead, roll the dice, turn him loose and see what happened next.

And what about Seth?

The thought of her brother had her taking a step back. If it was just her, she'd take the chance. But to take such a huge risk with Seth's future as collateral...

"All right. I'll give you the key." She braced for his reaction. "Just as soon as you promise me that when the weather improves you'll let me walk out of here, free and clear."

"Goddamn it, Genevieve, that's not fair—"

"None of this is," she cut him off sharply, zipping up her coat and slinging her scarf around her throat. Not waiting for his reply, since the last thing she wanted was for him to see the foolish tears suddenly stinging her eyes, she turned and walked toward the door. "Like I said, I'll be back."

She pulled open the door and stepped outside, welcoming the cold that immediately slashed into her like a razor-edged knife. Flipping up her collar, she struggled to get her breath as the sub-zero air burned her lungs.

Yet even as she trudged through the snow piled high on the porch and down the stairs, her thoughts were on the man inside. And what he would say if she told him the true reason for her sudden flight: That she was very much afraid she was falling hopelessly, irrevocably in love with him.

Jaw clenched, hands fisted, Taggart stalked a path parallel to the bed.

Damn, damn, *damn.* He'd just made what had to be his umpteenth search of every inch of cabin within his reach and he still couldn't find one stinking thing—not a bobby pin, paper clip or even a twist tie—that could possibly be used to pick the lock on the handcuffs.

Emotions churned through him. He was sick and tired of being a prisoner. Fed up with being chained like somebody's pet tiger. Up to his eyeballs with having to depend on St. Genevieve of the soft heart and luscious little body for every damn thing.

Sorry, pal. But even you've gotta admit, it's hard to steal a key or anything else off a woman who only gets near you when she's either naked or close to it.

One who, despite her soft-voiced concern and supposedly forthright manner, hadn't made one lousy mistake he could capitalize on.

And who was outside now, in the killing cold, taking unnecessary chances because he hadn't had the balls to lie and tell her what she wanted to hear. "Sure, baby. Give me the key and I'll not only let you go, I'll do anything else you want. You just name it—it's yours."

It would have been the expedient way to go, the smart thing to say. But when it came to Genevieve, words like *smart* and *expedient* didn't apply to him.

You've got that right. Whipped *and* enthralled *seem to be more your thing.*

The caustic thought shoved him over the edge. In a sudden fit of frustration, he snatched up the tray holding his empty breakfast dishes from the bed and hurled it across the room.

Shame had him by the throat even before the crockery struck the wall and shattered in a grinding explosion of sound.

What the hell was his problem?

What the hell *wasn't?*

Raking a hand through his hair, he stood stock still as he faced the demon driving him and reluctantly admitted it was him. That as a man whose self-restraint in every aspect of his life had always been paramount, he felt precariously out of control. And—the irony had his mouth twisting in a humorless smile—it was making him crazy.

Since meeting Genevieve, none of his behavior had been typical. From their first encounter out on the deck, when her unexpected bid to escape had resulted in the flying tackle that could have injured them both, to her recent insistence on venturing outside that he could have quashed with a few well-chosen words, he'd been one step behind and a few bricks shy of a full load.

He could remember, as a kid, his old man grumbling that no good deed ever went unpunished. Well, score one for Master Sergeant Richard Steele's life's-a-bitch-and-then-you-die take on life. And not because in the past few days his second son had been outwitted, imprisoned, beguiled and disarmed by a slip of a woman.

But because Taggart had broken the paramount rule of his life. He'd started to care about her.

Hell, who was he kidding? He hadn't *started* anything. He was solidly there. At some point when he wasn't looking—most likely because his brain had been in a sexual fog so complete he'd been rendered temporarily blind—Genevieve had crept right past his defenses and wedged a little sliver of herself deep into his heart that he was powerless to excise.

Not that it changed anything, he was quick to remind himself. He had an obligation to his brothers, to the Dunn family and to his own rapidly shrinking integrity to see this job through.

And if that wasn't enough of a reason to do what he was supposed to, there was Genevieve's long-term welfare to consider.

As much as it galled him, he had to admit she was pretty damn good at being a fugitive. But she could be the reincarnation of Mata Hari and it wouldn't matter. If she kept it up, it was just a matter of time before she got hurt.

Either she'd encounter a predator who'd use her isolation against her, or somebody with far fewer scruples than him would come after her in hopes of claiming some if not all of Steele Security's fee.

There was also the fact that the longer she was
AWOL, the deeper the hole she was digging for herself
with the judge whose order she'd defied in the first
place.

He could no longer avoid the truth. The sooner he
wrapped this up, the better for everyone, Genevieve included.

Cocking his head, he heard the faint crunch of boots
on snow that signified her return. He took a forceful
hold on his unruly emotions, shoving them back into
the sealed inner compartment where they belonged,
and tried to decide, as he tracked her progress up the
steps, just what he was going to say to her. He frowned
a little as there was a pause and he heard her say, "Oh,
for heaven's sake—"

And then her voice abruptly cut off, replaced with
the sound of crashing and rolling wood followed by an
alarmed cry, a muffled thump and then absolute, para-
lyzing silence.

"Genevieve!"
Genevieve had never heard another human being
actually roar, although the word was used in fictional
conversations all the time.

But it was exactly the way she'd describe the manner in which John was yelling her name.

Then again, she thought hazily, as she lay flat on her
back, desperately trying to suck in a breath to replace
the air that had been knocked out of her, *bellow* might
be an even better description. Although, come to think
of it, she didn't think she'd ever heard anybody do that,
either. Until now.

"Genevieve! Goddamn it, answer me!"

Gee. Talk about having your panties in a twist. Here she was suffocating, her vision starting to go dim, and he was having a major hissy fit, carrying on as if he'd slammed a drawer on his—

The thought was mercifully lost as the terrifying sensation of having a giant squatting on her chest abruptly vanished and she was finally able to drag a desperately needed breath into her starving lungs.

Except that it was colder out here than a Siberian meat locker, and the influx of icy air made her feel as if she'd inhaled a pissed-off porcupine.

Coughing and wheezing, she flopped onto her stomach and from there onto her elbows and knees, bringing her hands up to do what she could to warm the breath finally flowing in.

After what felt like an eternity, but was more likely a mere score of seconds, she decided she was going to live after all. And while she was likely to have a few bumps and bruises, she seemed for the most part to have survived unscathed.

She wasn't sure the same could be said of the cabin, she realized, as a loud crash came from inside. "*Genevi*—"

"I'm here," she called, doing her best to sound reassuring as she climbed gingerly to her feet. Encouraged by another quick inventory that found all her parts in working order, she picked up the hat she'd lost in the fall and did her best to dust the snow off it and whatever other areas of her clothing she could reach. "I'll be inside in a second. Don't worry."

Not worrying—about her discovery that she loved

him—was what *she'd* decided to do. Of course, first she'd had a minor meltdown courtesy of the bright and shiny new generator she hadn't been able to start. Then, when she'd realized her tears were freezing like sleet on her face, which wasn't a sensation she cared ever to repeat, she'd gotten a grip, taking a hard look at everything that had transpired between Taggart and herself.

It hadn't taken her long to realize that, while denying what she felt for him might make her feel better in the short run, it wasn't going to change anything in the larger scheme of things.

Yes, she hadn't known him very long. Yes, there was a host of things she didn't know about him. And yes, if she'd met him under different circumstances, she'd have deemed him too big, too tough and too intimidating to warrant a second look.

But none of that mattered now. She wasn't a person who gave her heart lightly or easily—that was obvious given that this was the first time she'd ever fallen in love. Sexually, she shared a bond with him she'd never felt with anyone else, while the chance to learn more about him made her feel like a kid at Christmas who'd been gifted with an abundance of presents.

As for his dangerous demeanor and aura of leashed power, she no longer found them threatening. She'd discovered he had too many honorable characteristics to offset them, including being committed to doing what he considered the right thing. They might be on opposite sides of the issue regarding Seth, he might break her heart by not returning her feelings, but she knew unequivocally that he'd never deliberately hurt her if there was any way he could avoid it.

The furnishings inside, on the other hand, sounded as if they were under a major assault. Wondering what on earth was going on, she blew out a breath, stomped as much of the snow off her boots as she could and walked through the door.

"My God." Her mouth formed a soundless O as she looked around. Not quite believing what she was seeing, she took in the easy chair that she'd placed next to the bed lying drunkenly on its side in the kitchen, the bright blue shards of broken dishes littering the hearth and, incredibly, the deep scars in the leg of the bed frame that anchored the far end of the chain.

Straining toward her at the opposite end of the chain was John, a bracelet of blood welling from the handcuff biting into his wrist. Her stomach dropped. "Oh, dear. What happened?" Scooting into the kitchen, she grabbed a clean towel and hurried toward him. "What did you do to yourself?"

"Me?" His expression savage, he caught her hand in a careful but inescapable grip as she reached to blot the blood from his wrist. "You just took a frickin' decade off my life."

"But you're bleeding."

He said something so profane it would have gotten his mouth washed out with soap in every foster home she'd ever lived in. "So are you."

"I am?" Confused, she followed his gaze to her hand, surprised as she saw the blood smearing her fingers and palm. "I don't think—"

"Be quiet." Taking the towel from her, he gently pressed it against her lips and chin, scowling as he lifted the red-stained cloth away and he surveyed her face. He blew out a breath. "It doesn't seem to be anything major. Looks like you bit your lip."

She blinked. Now that he mentioned it, her mouth did feel a little tender. Still, that didn't do a thing to explain—

She gave a startled squeak as without warning he peeled off her coat, unzipped her vest and began checking her out for further damage. "Really, I'm all right," she protested. "Which is more than I can say for this place—"

He made a sound as if he were grinding his teeth. "What the hell happened?" he demanded fiercely as he gently examined her arms and legs.

"Oh." She tried to ignore the little kernel of heat blooming shamelessly in response to his businesslike touch. "I fell. I caught the end of my scarf on one of the logs in the woodpile, tried to yank it free, then lost my footing getting out of the way when some pieces fell. I guess I went down kind of hard, because it knocked the wind out of me." She laughed unsteadily. "I think I actually saw a few stars."

His hands moved instantly toward her head, and it was then that it sank in how much she'd frightened him. Tenderness flooded her, and she reached up to intercept him.

"John." Linking her fingers in his, she waited for his gaze to meet hers. "I'm fine," she said softly. "Really."

For an instant his fierce expression didn't alter. Then, with the speed that always surprised her given his size, he pulled her into his embrace, cradling her against him as he rested his cheek on the top of her head.

With a sigh of contentment, she burrowed closer, basking in his strength and the glorious heat he radiated.

Then, just as quickly as he'd reeled her in, he was pushing her away. "Genevieve. Look at me."

He sounded so serious her heart gave a little thump of alarm as she tipped up her chin. "What? What is it?"

"I've decided to agree to your terms. Get this damn handcuff off me and when the time comes, I'll let you walk out of here with a forty-eight-hour head start."

"You will?"

That familiar muscle jumped once in his jaw and then was still. "Yeah." Cupping his hand around the back of her neck, he anchored his long fingers in her hair and tipped her head back for the gentle assault of his mouth. "Absolutely."

Ten

"This is nice." With a contented sigh, Genevieve shifted a little closer to Taggart as they sat on the couch by the fireplace.

Apparently there was a technique for constructing a blaze that actually gave off adequate heat, she mused, enjoying the warmth on her face as she gazed into the softly dancing flames. It was a discovery she'd made not long after freeing the owner of the broad shoulder she was currently nestled against.

In just a matter of hours, after first stripping her out of her damp outerwear, wrapping her in several blankets and depositing her in an easy chair with a book, John had put the cabin to rights, got the generator running, cleared the snow from the steps to the door, split a dozen logs into kindling and done his magic with the fire.

That hadn't been all. He'd put dinner together and done the dishes as well, and while Genevieve had found it all very impressive and endearing, his nonstop action had also driven home just how difficult being confined must have been for someone powered by such immense energy.

Happily, however, he now seemed as satisfied as she was to sit quietly and enjoy the night. For the first time in days, the wind had died to just an occasional gust, while the sky had cleared enough that a scattering of stars was visible. Beyond the frost-edged windows, the merest sliver of a silver moon peeked above the jagged silhouette of the mountain peaks looming on the horizon.

"Yeah, you're right. It is nice." Taggart traced the curve of her jaw with the pad of his thumb. "God knows, it beats the hell out of being shackled to the bed."

"Oh, I don't know. I'm sort of fond of that particular item of furniture. At least, when you're in it."

He turned his head to give her a quelling look.

She stared blandly back at him before returning her gaze to the fire. "Hey, I can't help it if I think there's something sexy about a guy in chains. At least when he's you, with that hard body and outlaw face—"

"Genevieve," he said warningly.

Virtuously, she quit talking. Then, unable to help herself, she glanced sideways at him, delighted when she saw the slight edge of embarrassment he was manfully trying to hide.

She swiveled her head toward him and widened her eyes. "Still, you do know it's true, right? I mean, women must come on to you all the time—"

"Genevieve."

She sighed and with a little pout turned back to the fire. "You know, I happen to be as fond of my name as the next person, but between you repeating it now, and all that earlier roaring and bellowing, I think you've about worn it out—"

She glanced sideways to see how she was doing and found herself squarely in the crosshairs of his visual sights. Only now there was a glint in his slightly narrowed eyes that warned he was on to her.

Deciding she'd pushed her luck as far as it would go, she raised an eyebrow. "Too much?"

"Oh, yeah."

"What gave me away?"

He raised an eyebrow of his own. "Outlaw face? Give me a break."

She gave an unapologetic shrug. "Hey, it sounded good when I read it in a book. And you have to admit, it did take you a while to catch on." She gave in to the impish grin she could no longer contain.

For the longest moment his reproachful expression didn't change. Then without warning, he caved. With a faint shake of his head, he finally let his mouth curve in a crookedly charming smile.

It was the best gift he could have given her. With a soft sigh of satisfaction, she shifted around and kissed him, treasuring the unfamiliar upturned tilt of his lips.

Once again she felt passion flare between them, a banked fire that seemed to grow stronger with every hour they spent together. Yet rather than give in to it, this time when they finally stopped to take in air, she gathered her crumbling willpower and, after pressing a lingering kiss to the corner of his mouth, forced herself to sit upright and move a few inches away.

"You okay?" he asked quietly, a flicker of disquiet in the green eyes meeting hers.

She reached out and brushed a tendril of his thick, straight hair off his forehead. "Of course. But there's something I'd like to talk to you about."

He looked the slightest bit wary for an instant, then his expression smoothed out. "All right."

She considered how best to start, and then realized that like most things, just being forthright was the way to go. "I want to tell you why I think Seth is innocent. And I want you to listen."

"Genevieve—"

"I know." She raised her hand in a plea for patience. "All the evidence points to him. And you think I'm acting out of blind devotion."

"You're right. I do. Hell, having brothers of my own, I even admire your loyalty. But at some point you've got to face reality—"

"Please, John. Just hear me out."

His lips thinned momentarily, but then he relented. "Okay."

She breathed a sigh of relief. "I do love Seth. I also think I know him better than anyone else since I helped raise him. I know—I *know*—he's not capable of what he's accused of. He might be able to kill in self-defense, or to protect me or someone else he loved, but for money? Never.

"However—" she sent him a quelling look when it looked as if he were going to interrupt "—that's not the only reason I know he's innocent. There's also the fact that, despite what everyone thinks, he didn't have a motive."

She stopped to take a breath, and to his credit, Taggart simply waited for her to continue.

She gathered her thoughts. "Four days before he died, Jimmy told Seth he was going to change his will and his life insurance, making Laura, his fiancée, his beneficiary. He planned to do it the next day. Not only that—" she spoke a little faster since she could sense Taggart's sudden exasperation with what he clearly considered her naiveté at accepting at face value her brother's version of anything "—but Seth also had no reason to hurt Jimmy because *I'd* already agreed to lend him the money to bail out the ski shop."

"What?"

She nodded. "I told this all to the police, but they didn't believe me. I suppose I can't blame them too much, since all they've got is my word on it. I had part of the money in savings—" which had since gone to Seth's attorney "—and I intended to borrow the rest. But Silver's a small town and, because I deposit the bookstore's receipts several times a week, I knew the bank's loan officer was out on a family emergency. I was just waiting for his return to make the arrangements.

"Obviously, there's no way I can prove that," she said earnestly. "Except *I* know that I'm telling the truth, and that means Seth didn't have a motive."

Shifting, Taggart stretched out his legs and mulled it over for a minute. "So we're back to the mysterious stranger theory?"

"No. I don't think so. I've had a lot of time to think

about it, and I think Seth's wrong. I don't believe Jimmy just happened to be carrying the gun and had the misfortune to walk in on something. That explanation relies on too many coincidences. I think somebody took the gun from his house, and either waited for him at my place or followed him there. I think he was killed on purpose."

To her relief, he didn't instantly shoot her down. "Okay, but why? From what I understand, he was a nice kid."

"He was." She felt the familiar ache, but saw no reason to go into how much she'd cared about Jimmy, how much he'd been like a second little brother. When this was finally all over, when Seth was safe, *then* she'd allow herself to mourn.

Taggart, however, seemed to sense her sadness, and settled her back into the curve of his arm. "But?" he prompted.

"But I read a lot, including mysteries and true crime stories, newspapers and magazines, and most of the time when someone's murdered, the crucial question is who gains from the victim's death."

"Which in this case happens to be Seth," he said quietly.

"Yes. But as I just explained, Seth believed just the opposite. And even if he didn't, even if he thought he was still Jimmy's beneficiary, he didn't need that money—which he probably wouldn't have received in time to save his business anyway—because he knew I was going to help him out."

He sifted the ends of her hair through his fingers and slowly blew out a breath. "Okay. But going with your theory, who other than Seth stood to profit from Dunn's death? The fiancée?"

She shook her head. "No. She's not my favorite person, but in her defense, I didn't know her long before all this happened, and despite what Jimmy told Seth, nothing was left to her. Besides, she has a pretty good alibi—she and her brother were with Jimmy's parents, waiting for him to show up so they could have dinner."

"Then who?"

"I don't know," she admitted.

He must have heard the dejection in her voice, because he gathered her closer as they both lapsed into silence. To her surprise, he was the first to breach it.

"I'm not sure what I think at this point," he said slowly, choosing his words with care. "I'm no cop, but I do know you're not going to solve anything being on the run. The longer you defy the court, the worse you're making things for yourself—and I'm pretty damn certain that's tough as hell on your brother.

"Still, the bottom line is that sometime in the future you *will* be going back, whether you want to or not. It wouldn't hurt for you to consider that it might be easier if you had somebody you could trust at your side."

Like him. Even though he didn't say it, his meaning was clear. Not certain what she felt—disappointed that he hadn't endorsed her theory about the murder, frustrated that despite his earlier promise he still clearly intended to come after her when her forty-eight hours were up, or moved by his offer to stand by her—she sighed. "I guess we both have some things to think about," she said softly.

"Yeah." Linking the fingers of one hand with hers,

he drew her onto his lap and brushed his lips over her temple. "I guess we do."

He remained still for a moment, and then his mouth began a lazy slide lower, pausing to bestow kisses on the corner of her eye, the top of her cheek, the edge of her mouth.

"Although," she said as she shifted to provide him easier access, unable to stifle an "oh" of appreciation when she felt him growing hard in reaction, "I suppose we don't have to do it right this minute."

"No." In a single deft move, he wrapped an arm around her and twisted, neatly positioning her underneath him. "I don't suppose we do."

The nightmare came near dawn, creeping into Taggart's sleep like deadly tendrils of smoke slithering under a doorway.

For one endless second, he felt the horror slyly twine itself around him. Then he was dragged away from Genevieve's comforting warmth and sucked deep into the bottomless abyss of the past, only to be spat out high in the Hindu Kush, the brutally beautiful mountain system that rose like a crown atop northern Afghanistan.

He'd been here before and knew what was coming. Knew, dreaded and despaired, yet was powerless to save himself from reliving the event that had nearly destroyed him.

It was a beautiful early-summer night. Stars spangled the vast bowl of the sky, while desolate spears of rock rose like a jagged picket line on either side of the steep, twisting defile that was the Zari Pass. A new moon hovered overhead, painting the landscape with eerie light.

As in every other nightmare before this, Taggart was both observer and participant.

Even as he hovered nearby and watched himself, he also felt the familiar weight of the pack on his back, the comforting shape of the M-16 in his hands, the slight burn in his lungs from the thin mountain air. He felt the rocky ground under his feet and heard the occasional murmured comment from another member of the unit through his headset.

"So what do you think, J.T.?" His lieutenant's quiet voice floated back to him on the breeze as the other man unexpectedly bypassed his mike.

"I don't know, Laz," he answered quietly and also off-mike.

Usually he walked point, since he preferred being out in front of the team, his senses strung tight, knowing that whatever happened the enemy would have to get by him first.

Tonight, however, he'd taken the tail, so he could help the CO keep an eye on Caskey, the new kid who was sandwiched between them.

A fatal mistake, the watching part of himself knew. If he had the lead, the coming tragedy wouldn't happen. He wouldn't allow it.

Still, to his credit, the him at the back of the pack sensed…something. Yet a glance up the track where Bear, Willis, Alvarez and the rest of the guys were strung out ahead of them like floats on a fishing line revealed nothing out of place.

He went with his gut anyway. "I can't put my finger on it, but it just doesn't feel right."

"Yeah. I'm getting that, too." With the decisiveness

that typified him, the other man thumbed on his mike so everyone could hear him. "Team, this is Alpha. Listen up, guys. We're packing it in for the night. We'll set up camp at that bend in the trail a quarter mile back."

"Sweet," Willis remarked, making the word into two syllables with his lazy Alabama drawl. "'Cuz I aim to tell you, sir, this place is creepin' me out. Plus I gotta take a leak."

"Again?" Alvarez's snort of good-natured disgust was pure east L.A. "Man, what is your problem? You must have a bladder the size of a friggin' thimble."

"Yeah? Well that still makes it way bigger than your—"

Whatever part of his teammate's anatomy Willis intended to insult was lost forever as he lowered his gun, reached for his fly and took a handful of steps toward the edge of the trail.

Without warning, a ferocious blast went off, flinging him up into the air.

For what seemed like an eternity, the young communications expert seemed to hang in the air, his body silhouetted by the glare from the land mine's explosion. His agonized wail shrieked through his mike until he abruptly crashed to the ground and went mercifully silent.

In the next instant the night disintegrated into a thousand disparate pieces, blown apart as the team was hit by a barrage of enemy fire that seemed to come out of nowhere.

Taggart registered the whistle of incoming rocket-propelled grenades; the staccato cough of automatic weapons fire; the deeper pop of older, Turkish-made bolt-action rifles. The smell of gunpowder and cordite filled his nostrils, along with the coppery scent of fresh blood.

Laced through that devil's brew were the shouts as men scrambled for cover, followed by screams as their paths intersected with the rest of the landmines slyly hidden along the trail's outer perimeters. Like human dominos set into motion by the hand of hell, his second set of brothers toppled one after the other.

Hunkering down to return fire, he heard himself shout, "Damn it, Caskey, *no!*" but it was too late as the younger man bravely raced forward toward the source of the incoming fire, only to be slammed back a dozen feet by a hail of gunfire.

In a series of freeze-frames burned forever on his mind, he saw Laz go down, too, then felt a scalding rush of relief as he heard his friend curse through the headset and realized he was only wounded.

"Hold on!" he shouted, ignoring the bullets he sensed whizzing past as he scrambled forward.

"J.T.?" Laz's amplified breathing was labored. "Get the hell out of here, *now!* That's an order."

"No way." Reaching the other man, he hefted Laz in a fireman's hold, swiveled back around and began to run. "Hang on. You just hang on, damn it," he ground out, too hyped on fury, fear and the resultant overload of adrenaline even to register that he was carrying two-hundred-plus pounds as he sprinted full out. "We're gonna be fine."

All he had to do was make it to that hairpin twist in the trail that Laz had mentioned, and he knew he could hold off whatever the enemy threw at him. And praise God, it wasn't that far away now, he was only a stone's throw away—

The flash of the RPG hitting the totem of rock to his right was blinding. He felt the concussion roll over him a second before the sound reached his ears, and then he was flying, tumbling through an endless darkness, falling down, down, down, knowing he was dead since he couldn't even hear his own desperate screams—

"John? *John.* Listen to me. It's okay. You're okay."

The woman's faraway voice whispered through the dark, a glimmer of light breaking through the blackness of his despair.

"Wake up. You're having a dream."

An angel? No. Angels didn't exist in hell. What's more, that voice, and the comfort and peace it promised, felt familiar somehow. As if she'd held off the dark and given him refuge before...

"Come on, wake up now, John. It's just a dream. A bad dream. You're safe."

Genevieve. He snapped his eyes open and was abruptly assaulted by the sound of his own harsh breathing, the taste of blood from having bitten his tongue, the sour stench of fear rising off his sweat-slick skin.

Shivering violently, he stared up at her propped above him, her eyes dark with worry. Saw her hand come down to soothe him, and instinctively reached out to block it. "*Don't.*"

"But—"

"Just give me a minute." He waited for her hand to withdraw, then squeezed his eyes shut and, ignoring the fact that his guts felt as if he'd just bungee jumped off the Empire State Building, concentrated on the simple act of breathing.

Time spun away. He wasn't sure how long it took

him to clamp down on his emotions, to banish the ghosts of Laz and Willis and the others, to will away the shakes, although it probably wasn't even a minute.

However long it was, when he finally opened his eyes, he had himself firmly under control. "Sorry," he said, reaching down deep to dredge up a rueful smile.

"Are you all right?"

"I'm fine. Just a bad dream, like you said. Had me going pretty good there, but I'm okay now."

Despite his assurance, the concern didn't leave her face. "Are you sure?"

"Yeah."

"Do you want to talk about it?"

"No." Somehow he managed not to flinch as she laid her hand on his cheek. "You know how it is. Even if it wasn't already fading, I probably couldn't explain it."

For a moment longer she continued to search his face, as if she knew damn well he was lying. He braced, fully expecting her to call him on it, but to his profound relief, she seemed to accept what he'd said at face value.

"Okay. If you're sure," she said softly, settling back down and laying her head on his shoulder.

"I am." He gave her arm a reassuring squeeze. "It'll be light soon. Try to get back to sleep."

"You, too."

"Sure." Even as he said it, he knew it wasn't going to happen.

So it wasn't any great surprise to be lying awake, watching the darkness in the room gradually lighten, long after her breathing had deepened into the sound sleep of the good and the righteous.

It was the kind of sleep he hadn't experienced since that night in the Hindu Kush when every member of his unit had died.

Everyone but him.

Eleven

Genevieve watched through the kitchen window as Taggart chopped wood like an automaton. Feet spread, shoulders bunching beneath the clean denim shirt and dark-green down vest he'd retrieved from his bag that morning, he appeared impervious to the spectacular beauty of the day.

Instead of taking time to appreciate the brilliant sunshine that made the snow sparkle like diamond dust, or looking up long enough to notice the lone eagle riding the thermals like a teenager out for a joyride, he wielded the ax with an unrelenting rhythm that was exhausting to watch.

At the rate he was going, they'd soon have more kindling than logs. Not that she cared. Wood was wood, and whatever its size it would burn.

She had far more pressing matters on her mind. Like whether John was out there for the exercise the way he claimed. Or if, as she suspected, his real goal was to keep her at arm's length.

Despite his reassurance of the previous night that he was fine, which he'd doggedly repeated again this morning, she knew he wasn't. Before he'd escaped outside, she'd had ample time to see the strain around his mouth, hear the detachment in his voice he couldn't entirely hide, practically *touch* the barrier he'd thrown up around himself.

If that wasn't enough to clue her in, being on the receiving end of his too-frequent smiles—which never quite reached his eyes—was.

She wondered if he had any idea he talked in his sleep.

With a slight shudder, she recalled the heartbreaking sound of his despair that had jolted her from sleep. His mumbled narrative may have been too disjointed for her to glean exact details, the when or where or how or why, but she'd heard enough to know he'd been in some sort of firefight that hadn't gone well. Men had died. Men he'd cared about.

It was also clear he'd sooner have his tongue extracted through his nose than share what had happened. Although she'd taken pains to keep her voice mild and her expression composed, simply asking if he wanted to talk had triggered a response similar to a heavily fortified gate slamming shut.

One moment he'd been there with her, haunted and hurting; in the next, the essence that made him the man she loved had been securely locked away behind an unbreachable wall.

Genevieve tapped a distracted finger against the kitchen counter.

She might not be able to get him to open up, but surely there was something she could do to stop his brooding and put an end to his self-inflicted isolation.

She stood there a moment longer, considering the golden gift of the sunshine, the heavenly blue of the sky, the pristine expanse of the snow, and realized the eagle had it right.

It was a day made for play. And while she might not be able to get through John's defenses, she thought she might know a way to get him to lower them all by himself.

Wasting no time, she gathered her snow gear, pulled it on, then slipped outside. Unconcerned with detection, since John was so absorbed in pulverizing another log he probably wouldn't notice if a flying saucer touched down beside him, she picked her spot and made her preparations.

When she was ready, she dusted off her palms, hefted one of her arsenal of snowballs in her hand and waited until her target was positioning the next log for its execution. The instant he straightened, she took a steadying breath, wound up for the throw and let loose.

Bull's-eye! She allowed herself a second of satisfaction as her missile struck Taggart squarely between the shoulder blades and sent a spray of snow shooting up to lodge at the back of his neck.

Ducking back around the cover of the stairs, she watched as he dropped the ax handle and spun around. "What the—"

She popped out and hurled snowball number two before he could complete the sentence. Unfortunately, her aim was off this time so she missed him entirely, the icy orb whistling harmlessly past his ear.

He scowled, clearly not amused. "Knock it off, Genevieve. I'm not in the—"

"Oh, jeez." She winced as her third try went high, hitting him in the chin instead of the chest. Yet the look of disbelief on his face as snow showered him, coating him from eyebrows to lips, was priceless. She didn't even try to hold back the laugh that rolled out of her.

He reached up, wiped himself off with his gloved hand. "You think that's funny?" he demanded, his narrowed eyes as green as his vest.

"As a matter of fact—" Wham! To her delight, this time she got him smack in the open neck of his shirt "—I do."

He swore, apparently not enjoying the sensation of ice-cold snow mixing with the sweat he'd worked up with the ax.

"You wanna know what else?"

"What?" While he sounded mightily aggravated, he couldn't entirely suppress the slight twitch at one corner of his mouth.

She took it as a hopeful sign. "The way you're getting all pissy? I think that makes you what my friend Arnold calls a girlie man."

Her gleeful insult did it.

He was moving before she had time to blink, easily dodging the snowball she tossed hastily his way as she gave a shriek and bolted away. Forced to stick to the path he'd carved on his trips to the shed, she was an easy target as he scooped snow up by the handfuls as he ran.

Wadding it together, he peppered her with a series of hits that came one after the other in the short time it took him to catch up with her.

Then his arms came around her and he lifted her off her feet. She laughed breathlessly as they tumbled to the ground, her relief as she saw a smile finally flit across his face mixed with tenderness as he took care to absorb the brunt of their fall.

The second they quit skidding across the icy ground he flipped her onto her back, caged her in with his elbows, and made a show of glowering down at her. "Laugh all you want, angelface," he growled. "You're in serious trouble now."

Angelface. The endearment made her feel warm all over. She did her best not to let on, however. "Ohhh," she hooted, "aren't you the big bad."

Much as he had the previous night, he gave it his best shot but couldn't quite sustain his dark and dangerous look. "Big bad?" A tiny V of disbelief formed between his eyebrows. "Where the hell do you come up with this stuff?"

Willing to forgo her dignity and act silly if it would keep his demons at bay for even a little while, she shook her head. "Forget it. No way am I telling you all my secrets."

"You're not, huh?"

"Not a chance."

"Yeah, well, we'll see about that." Pinning her in place with one big hand, he scooped up a handful of snow with the other. His gaze raked her front, zeroed in on her waist where she'd run up the double zipper to allow herself greater freedom of motion, then came back to her face. The smile he finally unleashed on her wasn't nice.

"Don't you dare."

"Yeah, like I'm going to feel threatened by you."

"John—"

"Too late." Releasing her long enough to shove up the hems of her shirts, he clapped the icy mass in his hand against her bare stomach.

"Ohmi—" Gasping, protesting and laughing, she bucked and twisted, doing her best to shake him off.

She might as well have been trying to shift a bulldozer.

Changing tactics, she wrapped her arms around his neck and her thighs around his hips, figuring if she was going to suffer he might as well share the pain.

Surprise, surprise. He really *was* the big bad. Or at least the big, she amended, as she registered the solid length of his arousal pressed eagerly against her.

Her gaze flashed to his face to find his eyes riveted on her with such desire in their mossy depths it stole her breath. "Oh, John," she said softly, her amusement ebbing as everything she felt for him filled her up and took its place.

"Yeah," he murmured in the instant before his arms came around her and his mouth settled hungrily over hers.

His lips were cold and tasted of snow. His kiss was hot and greedy. Genevieve sank into it, welcoming the avid thrust of his tongue, glorying in this further proof that he wanted her. She could feel his heart pounding, despite their layers of clothing, and the knowledge that she had such an effect on him thrilled and enthralled and humbled her.

When he shifted onto his knees, scooped her into his arms, climbed to his feet and headed for the cabin, she didn't protest.

She wanted him and anything—everything—he was willing to give.

"I've never made love during the day before," Genevieve said softly, watching Taggart undress as she knelt naked on the bed.

Being here with him, like this, at this time of day, felt different, she mused. Daring and a little risqué and incredibly intimate. There were no shadows to hide in, no escape from the shafts of glittering sunshine striping the room and painting everything they touched a pale, shimmering gold.

"I have," he volunteered unexpectedly, peeling off his shirt to reveal the wide, smooth shoulders and sculpted chest that never failed to put a hitch in her breath. "Once."

Amazed that he'd willingly share such information, she told herself to concentrate, even as her pulse tripped. She'd never seen him completely naked in broad daylight, she realized. "How was it?"

He unsnapped his jeans and slid the zipper down. With an economy of motion that was laudable, he stripped off his jeans and briefs together. "Fast." The look he tossed her way was unexpectedly rueful. "I was sixteen."

"Ah." The thought of him as a teenager made her wistful. She wondered what he'd been like, if he'd been open and hopeful for the future. But no, she realized an instant later. By then he'd already lost his mother and been shipped away from home to military school.

It made her want to gather him close, protect him, keep him from ever feeling more pain, even though she knew not only that it was impossible, but that he'd never allow it. He had too much pride to let her or anybody else shelter him.

"What?" he said, searching her face as he stretched out beside her.

"Nothing. I just…" Chiding herself for putting concern in his voice, she smiled. "This was one of your better ideas, that's all." Coming up on her knees, she saw his surprise as she braced her hands on either side of him, then lowered her head and pressed an open-mouthed kiss to the shallow oval of his navel.

This—the gift of pleasure—was something he would accept, and was well within her power to bestow.

Deliberately leaving the best for last, she ignored the velvety thrust of his straining arousal and slowly skimmed her lips over the washboard ripple of his abdomen. He had the most magnificent body she'd ever seen, and truth be told, having it stretched out like this for her delectation made her feel all fizzy inside.

Taking her time, she explored with her hands and her mouth. She trailed her fingers over every inch of those glorious abs first, then the curves of his pectorals from his sides to his middle. She flicked her tongue over the hardened bead of his nipple, delighted to hear a soft sound rumble from his throat. Intrigued, she did it again, and felt his hand slide into her hair a moment before he tugged her head up.

"Genevieve," he said, his voice smoky, his eyes dark with a look she'd never seen in them before.

"What?" With a pinch of concern, she reached up, touched her hand to his face. "What is it?"

"I want—" He stopped, and she saw his struggle to get out the words. "I need to see your face when I'm inside you."

The words alone were enough to trigger a liquid flutter inside her. It got stronger as he slid his hand around and traced her lips with his thumb. "Now," he said hoarsely.

"Yes." Scooting up, she claimed his mouth, giving herself over to him completely as he held her close and reversed their positions.

In a blink of an eye, the kiss went from soft and tender to greedy and heated. In the next instant, he was tearing his mouth away, holding himself still for the heartbeat it took her to open her eyes. Then he plunged inside her.

She was wet, slick and yielding, more than ready, and she could feel herself stretching to accommodate his considerable size as he began to pump. His hips slowly pistoned as they continued to watch each other, their gazes locked.

He was so beautiful, she thought, as the first ribbon of pleasure made an immediate arrival and curled through her. From that strong, austere face to his wide palms and long fingers, from the warm, corrugated surface of his stomach to the powerful, lightly haired thighs wedged now between her smooth, softer ones, he was utterly, quintessentially male.

Never in her life had she been so aware of being female, of the fundamental drive to claim and be claimed by a man.

Not any man, she amended as she felt herself slide a little closer toward completion, that single ribbon of toe-curling sensation having given birth to a silken web that had her firmly in its grip.

Just John. Only John. Always John.

She watched, enthralled, as his eyes began to blank and his breathing quicken as his control started to evaporate. Teeth clenched, perspiration misting his skin, he shifted, sharpening the angle of penetration and began to drive. "Damn it," he gasped. "I can't— I can't hold back."

"It's all right," she whispered, her head going light as pleasure began to squeeze her.

Nothing in her life had prepared her for this, she thought hazily. The delicious heat of his big body. The raw, drugging sensuality of the act they were sharing. Her own wildly eager response.

Emotion overran her as if she were the top wine flute in a champagne fountain. It was too much to contain. Too precious to hoard.

Reaching up, she dug her hands into his hair, rising up to meet him at the same time that she tugged his head down to hers. "I love you, John," she said clearly, her gaze never leaving his. Clamping around him with sleek, inner muscles, she felt herself reaching, reaching… "Come with me," she implored.

He quivered as if she'd struck him. Then his eyes squeezed closed and his mouth crushed down on hers, a welcome marauder.

Every muscle in his big body shuddering, he held on to her as if she were his only anchor as the storm broke and pleasure swept them away.

Twelve

"**Y**ou shouldn't do that," Taggart said quietly, his shoulders still heaving as he sat up and swung his feet to the floor.

"Do what?" Genevieve said blankly to his back.

He heard the sheets rustle and knew she'd sat up. "Say things you don't mean."

"Like I love you?" There was a telling pause, and then she said evenly, "Pardon me, but I think I know my own mind."

Frustrated, he twisted around to face her. The last thing he wanted was to hurt her; why couldn't she just acknowledge she'd spoken in the heat of the moment and let it go? "You're wrong. You're confusing great sex with…something else."

"Trust me. I know the difference between the two."

Her expression was serene as she met his gaze. "And I didn't tell you because I was hoping you'd say it back or because I'm looking for a commitment, if that's what's bothering you. I just wanted you to know. Love, freely given, is a gift, John. Not a burden. Or at least it shouldn't be."

How the hell was he supposed to respond to that? Feeling all tied up inside and hating it, he stood, scooped up his jeans and yanked them on, then paced to the window and stood looking blindly out. "There are things you don't know about me."

"You're right. It's also true that if you only count the time in hours, we haven't known each other very long. But none of that matters. I feel closer to you than I've ever felt to anyone except Seth. And I trust my judgment. I know you, John. Maybe not every little detail, but the things that are important. I know you care— about your brothers, your job, about doing the right thing. I know you light me up inside. I know you're a good man."

"Oh, yeah?" He wheeled around, surprised to find she'd flown under his radar once again and was standing just a few feet away, wrapped in his shirt. "What if I told you nine guys are dead because of me?"

"I wouldn't believe you."

He turned back to the window, the sunshine unable to touch the endless winter that lived inside him. "Then you'd be deluding yourself."

"No," she said firmly.

"*Yes,* damn it." He told himself just to shut up and let it go, but now that he'd gone this far, he couldn't seem to stop the words from flowing out of his mouth.

"You know I was a Ranger. My last deployment was to northern Afghanistan. My unit had been there nine months when word came down from CentCom that they had reliable intel an old trade route was being used as a pipeline by terrorists coming in from Pakistan. We were ordered to check it out.

"The trip out took a week, but there was zilch to indicate that anybody but us had been over that pass in years." He took a shallow breath and an iron grip on the bitter emotions burning his throat. "Until we started back. It was night, we were maybe two days from our base camp, pushing it a little because heavy rains earlier in the day had slowed us down. One minute everything was fine."

Willis's amused drawl whispered through his mind but he shook it off.

"The next, we were taking heavy fire, with nowhere to hide because the trail had been mined since we'd come through. The whole thing lasted five, maybe ten minutes. When it was over—" he shrugged "—I was the only one left."

"Dear God." Her face, always so expressive, was a telling mixture of shock and horror.

Taggart told himself he ought to be glad; after all, wasn't this what he'd wanted? For her to see him as the bastard he really was?

Damned right it was.

So why did he feel as if he'd just lost a vital piece of himself? Something he wasn't sure he could go on without?

"How—" Genevieve swallowed. "However did you survive?"

He smiled humorlessly. "I was carrying my CO, who'd been hit, when a grenade went off beside us. He took the brunt of the blast; I got blown over a cliff. I got lucky—" the word felt like acid on his tongue "—and hit a ledge about a hundred feet down."

Genevieve tried to picture it in her mind; the noise and the confusion and the urgency and the fear, and then what must have seemed like an unending fall. That was the memory, she now realized, that must have prompted his agonized cries at the end of his nightmare. The ones that had sent shivers down her spine and pushed her even harder to wake him up.

She drew in a deep breath, blew it out, fought for composure as her heart broke just a little more for him. "How badly were you hurt?"

He shrugged dismissively. "I was a little banged up from the fall."

"Define *banged up*."

His mouth set stubbornly, and she knew before he answered that he was going to lie. Clearly, the last thing he wanted was sympathy, of any kind. "Nothing major. I told you. I was lucky, remember?"

She heard the self-loathing in his voice, and suddenly it all made sense. The air of isolation; the tightly controlled emotions; the stubborn, misplaced conviction that he didn't deserve to be loved. "What did you do?"

"I climbed up the cliff, checked to see if anyone else was alive." His voice was suddenly uninflected, his expression cool, as if what he was saying was of no significance whatsoever. Genevieve didn't buy it for a minute. "All our comm units were shot to hell, so I had to wait to radio for help until I got back to camp."

He'd said they were two days out. She pictured him—injured, since no one could fall that far and escape damage to their body—with no one to talk to about the carnage he'd witnessed or the friends he'd lost. And she ached for his pain and despair.

It took all of her control not to give in to the urge to step close, wrap her arms around him, offer what comfort she could.

Yet with an instinct she didn't question, she knew that if he were to have any chance of healing, he had to confront the guilt that had clearly festered inside him for far too long. She took a deep breath. "And all of this is your fault...how?"

His mouth twisted. "We never should have been there in the first place. I knew—something felt off right from the beginning. Unlike CentCom, we were there, on the scene. If there'd been hostiles passing through the area, there would've been whispers in the villages, something passed along from one of our contacts."

Although she suspected she knew the answer, she asked the question anyway. "So why didn't you say something?"

"I did. But I should have recognized that it was a setup, raised hell, even refused to go—"

"And disobey orders?" she said in disbelief. "You couldn't do that. Any more than you could have lived with yourself if you'd hung back while your unit was about to walk into a situation you thought was dangerous."

"Listen, for God's sake. Maybe you're right about that, but what happened on that pass— It was just all...wrong. Teams get used to a certain pattern, into a kind of rhythm, on patrol. I should've been in front, the way I usually was, but instead I was hanging back at the rear—"

"Why? Were you sick or injured or something?"

"No. I was keeping an eye on—what the hell does it matter? The point is I wasn't where I should've been—"

"And if you had been up front, what would that have accomplished?" she demanded. "Were you so much better than the man taking your place that you could have prevented an ambush?"

"No, but—I—" He stopped, regrouped. "That's not—" He stopped again, and just stared at her.

"You're not psychic, John. If you were, you wouldn't have spent the past few days chained to the bed. Obviously your instincts were right, but it was your job, your unit's job, to do exactly what you did, to take that walk into danger no matter how you felt. The responsibility for what happened rests with the men who attacked you and whoever higher up your chain of command okayed the information about the pass in the first place."

Unable to stand the physical distance between them another second, she padded close, rucked back the sleeves of his shirt and reached up to cup his face. "I'm sorrier than I can say that you suffered such a terrible loss." She thought about her grief for Jimmy and couldn't imagine what it must have been like for him. "But what happened wasn't your fault. You're not God. Or a superhero. And I'm sure as hell not sorry you're alive. I doubt any of the friends you lost that night would be, either. They'd be as glad as I am that you made it out."

Taggart gazed down into her face. He wasn't sure what he felt, what he thought; so many things were suddenly tumbling through his mind at once that he couldn't seem to get a grip on any particular one.

What he did know was that, while he wasn't convinced Genevieve's assessment of his actions was correct, she clearly believed what she'd said with every fiber of her being. And because she did, a part of his heart that had been so damn cold since that devastating night on Zari Pass four years ago felt warm again.

What's more, as he felt her arms come around him in a fierce embrace, he realized that for the first time since he could remember, he didn't feel completely alone.

Standing on the prow of the deck, a steaming cup of coffee cradled in his hands, Taggart raised his face and soaked in the sun.

Some time during the night, a chinook had blown in. The soft breeze ruffled his hair with warm fingers while it set the surrounding evergreens gently swaying. It was as if, he mused, the immense trees were slow dancing to the music of the melting snow as it dripped from the trees, trickled off the cabin's eaves, raced merrily along dozens of narrow, winding rivulets toward the creeks and streams murmuring in the distance.

At the rate the thaw was progressing, the roads should be passable later that day.

That made it decision time.

In the past twenty-four hours he'd revealed things to Genevieve he'd never shared with another living soul. And instead of playing it safe and pushing him away, she'd opened her heart even wider and invited him to come closer.

What's more, in the wake of yesterday's painful disclosure, she'd somehow understood that he'd reached the limit of what he could emotionally process and she hadn't pressed him any further.

She'd led him back to bed instead, where they'd stayed, except for a brief raid on the kitchen long after the sky had darkened, making love with nothing held back. They'd gone slow, been wild. They'd shared tenderness, urgency, heated whispers, raw cries of passion. They'd kissed, clung, explored, feasted, turned each other inside out and held each other together.

He might not be in love with her, not exactly, but he felt more connected to her than he had to anyone since his mother died.

So how the hell could he betray her?

For the first time since he'd told her that he'd let her go in order to secure his own freedom, he admitted to himself that in the back of his mind he'd been reserving the right to renege on their deal. Every reason he'd cited at the time to justify why she'd be better off in custody still stood, with the added kicker that he felt even more protective now than he had before.

And yet… He couldn't stand the thought of destroying her trust. Despite the fact that he had an obligation to his brothers and the client who'd paid for their services, and that he truly felt it would be in Genevieve's best interest to turn herself in.

Hearing the door open and the sound of her footsteps approaching, he turned to watch her walk toward him. Dressed in dark jeans and a pale-pink sweater, her hair gleaming like burnished silk in the sun, she was beautiful. He wondered how he could ever have considered her merely pretty.

"You look far too serious for such a gorgeous day," she said lightly, joining him at the rail. Like a flower, she raised her face to the sun.

He shook his head. "It's the weather. It's hard to believe it can go from minus zero to fifty plus in less than forty-eight hours."

"Nature's just full of surprises," she agreed, shifting her gaze to him. "So are you."

Just for a second he thought he saw something in her eyes— But no. No way could she know what he'd been thinking, know about the internal battle he was waging over what was right and what was best. "You think so?"

"Uh-huh. Breakfast was wonderful. If I'd known you could cook like that—" her mouth turned up "—I'd have chained you to the stove instead of the bed."

"Huh. I'm not sure that's a compliment."

"No, really, it is. Although, now that I think about it, I take it back." She leaned bonelessly against him, gave a little sigh of contentment as his arm came around her. "Bed is definitely the best showcase for your talents."

He narrowed his eyes. "You do realize you're skating on really thin ice, right?"

She laughed, that soft, delighted chuckle that never failed to light him up inside. As the sound of it faded away, they simply stood on the deck together, wrapped in a companionable silence as they admired the day.

Then Genevieve gave a faint sigh. "The snow's melting off pretty fast."

"Yeah. But it's only temporary. Winter's definitely here. You can feel it in the air. Another few days and the cold and the snow will most likely be back."

"I don't suppose we could hang around for that?" she asked a trifle wistfully.

"No. I don't think we can." Steeling himself, he turned her in his arms, telling himself that the least he owed her was to look her in the eyes when he admitted he wasn't sure he could just let her walk away. "Listen—"

"I've—" she said at the same time.

They both stopped. He inclined his head. "Go."

"All right." She swallowed, then visibly steadied herself. "I've decided to release you from your promise."

For a second he was sure he hadn't heard right. "What?"

"If we start packing up right now, we should be ready to leave by this afternoon."

Stunned, he took a moment to wrap his tongue around the questions crowding his mind. "Are you sure?"

"Yes."

"But…why? What changed your mind?"

"I've been thinking about some of the things you said. About how I've done all I can, and how I'm making things even harder on Seth. And that if I go back now, with you, I won't be totally alone. That is—" she looked up at him and, for one of the few times he could remember, he could see both fear and uncertainty in her eyes "—if your offer still stands."

"Yeah, sure, but—Jesus, Genevieve." He shook his head with the vague thought that maybe that would help clear it. "I just don't get it. Yesterday, you were so adamant…."

Her expression changed, some of the tension draining away to be replaced by unmistakable tenderness. Reaching up, she laid her hand against his cheek. "You're not quite as inscrutable as you think," she said quietly. "And the longer I've had to think about it, the more I've come to realize that I've put you in an untenable situation.

"Besides—" she lightly drew her thumb over the seam of his lips, her throat visibly working as she struggled to hold on to her air of calm "—you trusted me enough to tell me what happened to you. How can I not trust you back?"

It was too much. At the same time that he felt a huge weight had been lifted from his shoulders, a part of him worried uneasily that she was making a serious mistake, that he wasn't worthy of such faith.

"Genevieve—"

"It'll be all right," she said firmly, once more seeming to read his mind.

"Damn straight." He'd see to it, or die trying, he vowed to himself. "I swear I'll do everything I can to expedite this whole thing, try my best to convince the judge to go easy on you—"

"I know you will. I trust you, remember?" She gave his arm a reassuring squeeze, then dropped her hand to her side and took a step away. "Now, I'm going to start packing things up, before I chicken out and change my mind."

And briskly turning away, she left him alone with nothing but the sunshine and his own unsettled thoughts for company.

Thirteen

"**M**y rig is *where?*" Taggart demanded, jiggling the keys to Genevieve's truck in his hand. After a very short discussion, they'd agreed his was the vehicle of choice in which to make the drive back to Colorado.

"In a barn about a mile and a half down the road from where you left it," she repeated patiently. Pausing in the task of emptying the contents of the fridge into a garbage bag, she picked a piece of paper up off the counter and proffered it to him. "Here. I've written down the directions and drawn you a map."

Taking the sheet from her, he studied it a moment, folded it and slid it into his pocket, then looked back up at her and shook his head. "You walked through the snow, in the dark, just to hide it?"

She widened her eyes, doing her best to look innocent. "I was keeping it safe for you."

"Yeah, right."

"Hey, a girl's got to do what a girl's—"

He expediently cut her flow of words by the simple act of tugging her into his arms. "Spare me the pitch," he murmured, lowering his head to rest his forehead against hers. "Bottom line, Bowen, you're a menace. How the hell you managed to make it this far—" shifting, he found her mouth and interspersed his next words with a series of erotic, unhurried kisses "—without serious injury—" his hands slowly stroked down her back as he caught her bottom lip between his teeth and bit down lightly "—is beyond me."

Genevieve felt her body start to hum. His simplest touch made her feel warm and malleable, like Silly Putty left out in the sun. "John?" she murmured, her eyelids drifting shut as his mouth slid over the curve of her jaw to explore her throat.

"Hmm?"

"If you don't go now, you won't be going at all."

"No?" Nothing happened for a moment, then his hands slowly relaxed their grip on her butt. Sighing, he met her heavy-lidded gaze with a rueful one of his own. "I suppose you're right."

She eased back, forcing herself to step away from his seductive warmth. "Yes. I am."

"All right. If you're sure you don't want—"

"*Go,*" she ordered with a breathless laugh. She watched as he strode across the room and out the door. Feeling mixed relief and regret, she started to turn back to the fridge when she abruptly remembered the distributor cap. "Wait!" she called, dashing after him onto the porch.

Already down the stairs, he stopped and turned. "What?"

"Just hang on a minute." Due to the amount of chopping he'd done the past two days, the wood pile was seriously diminished, which was good since it made her task easier. Leaning over the low stack of logs that were left, she reached down and cast about until her fingers closed over the bulbous piece of metal. Straightening, she twisted back around. "You'll need this." With a smooth, underhand toss, she lobbed it to him.

He snatched the shiny metal cap out of the air, spent a long second considering it, then once more looked up at her.

"If I'm ever in serious trouble, I want you guarding my back," he informed her dryly.

Genevieve smiled. As compliments went, it was first class and she didn't doubt it showed in her smile. "I love you, John Taggart Steele," she said softly, unable to stop herself. "Now go, so you can get back."

"Count on it." He headed for the truck.

It was done.

Standing with her back to the window, Genevieve took a slow look around the cabin's interior.

All of her things, plus John's modest bag, were packed and stacked neatly to one side of the door. The fridge was clean and unplugged, the few perishable foodstuffs that had been left bagged for disposal. She'd made sure the fire was out and closed the flue, flipped the breaker switch to the water heater and turned off the water valve under the sink. Since the power had come back on shortly after dawn and John had already dealt with the generator, she'd had only to make sure all the lamps and appliances were either turned off or unplugged.

In a gesture symbolic of her hopes for the future, she'd put clean sheets on the bed, and, in a reminder of the most life-altering week of her life, left the chain neatly coiled atop the smooth expanse of the comforter. She hoped that, when the next few days or weeks or—surely it wouldn't be more than months?—were over, she'd be able to convince John to return for a long getting-reacquainted weekend.

That is, if he still felt the way he did now when she got out of jail.

She wondered if she'd be allowed to see Seth, then realized it was unlikely. Suddenly unable to ignore the fear that had been plucking at her with icy fingers ever since she'd made the decision to turn herself in, she swallowed hard and admitted she didn't know what to expect. She'd never had so much as a traffic ticket, and, while she'd read countless books where people went to jail, the reality of actually being locked away, completely at the mercy of strangers, felt altogether different.

She just had to keep reminding herself that she wouldn't be alone. She hadn't lied when she'd told John she trusted him. And though she didn't share his optimism regarding what was about to happen—she'd known since she'd decided to run that the consequences would be grave—she'd get through it. She was young, strong, resilient, accustomed to looking out for herself.

And it wasn't as if she had a choice.

Still, it would certainly help if John would get the lead out and get back before she went from a mild case of cold feet to feeling frozen from the eyebrows down.

She glanced at the clock. He should have returned by now, she thought with a frown. Since the room felt as if it was starting to close in on her, she decided she might as well take her current book and wait outside in the sun. Just having a plan, however inconsequential, made her feel better, so she snatched up her paperback and the coat she'd laid on the couch.

She was halfway to the door when the knob started to turn.

Even as she felt a rush of relief that John was finally back, she faltered in midstep, a small alarm going off in her head as she realized that she hadn't heard him drive in.

In the next instant, the door crashed open and a tall, dark-haired stranger burst into the room.

Her heart seemed to stop as she found herself staring down the barrel of an enormous, dull-black gun. "On the floor! Now!" the intruder shouted at her. "Keep your hands where I can see them!"

She was so terrified she couldn't speak, much less move so much as an eyelash. Yet in the midst of her paralysis, time seemed to slow dramatically to the point where she registered every minuscule detail going on around her, from the pounding of more feet and the harsh cries of other male voices screaming at her to get down, to the striking features of the man now gripping her shoulder.

In the same instant that he spun her around and

forced her to the ground, she realized he bore an uncanny resemblance to John. Same inky hair, same height, same strong, straight nose and startling green eyes. His were a darker shade, however, and his features were more refined. Dressed as he was, all in black, including a long leather coat that hung to midcalf, he exuded a dangerous, fallen-angel sort of elegance.

Or would, she thought numbly, as he yanked her arms back and slapped a pair of handcuffs on her wrists, if he weren't scaring the wits out of her. Her state of mind didn't improve as she heard a swift double click of sliding metal a second before an unchambered bullet dropped with a ping on the floor inches from her face. She squeezed her eyes shut and the next thing she knew, he was patting her down, his hands skimming efficiently and impersonally over her.

Apparently satisfied she was unarmed, he rocked back onto his heels, dragged her to her knees and yanked her around to face him. "Where is he?" he demanded. Holding her upright with one powerful hand, he caught her chin in the other. "Talk to me, *Genevieve.* What the hell have you done to my brother?"

"John?"

His brows rose just for an instant. "That's right."

She tried to dredge up enough saliva so she could actually form an entire sentence. "He—" She had to stop, swallow, start over again. "He went to get his SUV." She forced herself to meet those intense emerald eyes without flinching. "He's fine. I swear. He should be back any minute."

The stare he sent her was lethal. "For your sake, you better be telling the truth."

"I am." For the first time, she started to get just the slightest bit angry. "If you'll just be patient, hold on a minute, you'll see for yourself—"

"Oh, you can count on that, sweetheart," he said grimly, effortlessly hauling her with him as he stood.

For the first time, she took note of the two other men in the room and her heart sank even lower. Unlike John's impeccably dressed brother, they were wearing uniforms that identified them as local sheriff's deputies.

Then to her horror, he gave her a slight shove toward the waiting officers. "Get her out of here," he instructed them. "Like I told your boss, somebody with the proper papers to take her back to Colorado should be at the airport by now. You can tell them I'll check in with them later."

"What about your brother?" the younger of her two guards asked. "You sure you don't want us to stay?"

"No. If he doesn't turn up in the next hour, you can bet you'll hear about it," he said, voice clipped.

Sending her one more frigid look that warned he'd meant what he'd said about her paying a steep price if John didn't turn up soon and in one piece, he turned his back and dismissed her with a single flick of one graceful, long-fingered hand.

Taggart tossed the tire jack next to the flat currently occupying the cargo hold of his rig. Closing the lift gate, he impatiently snapped the empty tire mount back into place and walked around and climbed behind the wheel.

He supposed he ought to be glad the damn tire had blown now, on a deserted mountain road where he'd been forced to keep his speed down, rather than later on the freeway when he'd have been going considerably faster.

But right at the moment, it didn't feel like much of a blessing, he reflected, as he restarted the SUV's engine, cranked the wheel and pulled back onto the road.

This entire excursion had already taken a ridiculous amount of time. While Genevieve's map had been fairly detailed, he'd still managed initially to miss the narrow track cut through a grove of sagging aspens that had eventually led him to the ramshackle barn where his SUV had been stashed.

There was just something about Genevieve, he mused. Even from a distance, she seemed able to scramble his circuits and knock him off balance. He wondered if he was doomed to spend the rest of his life a dime short and a step behind.

I love you. They were just three little words, but they'd been playing in a continuous loop in the back of his mind—and screwing with his concentration—ever since she'd said them back on the porch. It had given him more than enough time to reflect on just how desperately he wanted to hear them again.

Given the effort he'd made to get her to rescind them just a day before, there was a certain irony in that.

Yet merely this brief interlude away had made him realize how totally he'd come to need her in order to feel complete. Her quick mind, her quirky humor, her soft heart and melting touch—she was now as necessary to him as breathing. He might not have a label for his feelings, but he couldn't imagine his life without her, either, at least for the immediate future. She was the best thing to have happened to him in a very long time and he didn't intend to give her up.

Instead of jail, he'd decided to take her back to his place, enlist his brothers' help and see what sort of deal they could strike with the Silver County authorities. If that meant giving the retainer back to the client, so be it. He'd made a considerable amount of money the past few years and, since his needs were few, he had the resources to cover that as well as anything else that cropped up.

His hands tightened on the wheel a fraction as he imagined Genevieve's relief when he told her. An unfamiliar emotion swept through him and, though it took him a moment, eventually he recognized it for what it was. Anticipation. Something else he hadn't experienced in a very long while.

It vanished in a heartbeat, however, when he spotted the mud-splattered silver SUV parked on the far side of the turnoff to the cabin. Frowning, he slowed, prickles of uneasiness radiating down his spine as he took in the rental sticker on the back bumper.

Just what, he wondered, were the chances of somebody from out of town picking that spot to park out of countless miles of empty road?

And just like that he knew, even before he turned off the road onto the driveway and spotted the churned-up tracks in the snow and mud made by tires newer and wider than the ones on the old pickup he'd driven out.

Jaw set, he hit the accelerator, hands rock-steady as he took the slippery, twisting track at a speed that wasn't even remotely safe. Topping the final hill, he pushed the vehicle even harder, ignoring the thump as he fishtailed around the final curve and the loose tire in the back crashed against the wheel well.

He swore, his gut clenching, as he saw that the clearing beside the cabin was empty of vehicles, and he realized he was too late. Slamming on the brakes, he jammed the gearshift into Park and flung himself out the door while the big SUV was still rocking on its tires. Taking the steps in one powerful bound, he stormed across the porch and threw open the door.

Just as he'd expected, his older brother was the sole occupant of the room. "Goddamn it, Gabe, what the hell have you done?" he demanded, advancing menacingly on the other man as if the gun that had made an appearance at his explosive arrival didn't exist. "Where is she?"

Gabriel gave him a careful once-over, the tension edging his face ebbing away as he apparently saw for himself that Taggart was fine. "Good to see you, too, bro," he said mildly. His movements calm and deliberate, he removed the clip from the gun and uncocked the slide, then slid the weapon back into the holster hidden by his coat's custom fit.

"Where the hell is Genevieve?" Taggart repeated.

"Right this minute?" Gabe shot his cuff to glance at the deceptively simple stainless-steel watch gracing his wrist. "Most likely winging away from the Kalispell airport in the plane with the armed escort that the Silver County prosecutor sent for her."

Taggart decked him. Without stopping to think, for the first time since he'd been thirteen and Gabe fourteen, and they'd had their last major disagreement over the wisdom of his plan to steal cars for a living, he socked his big brother in the mouth with enough force to knock him to the floor.

Wisely, Gabriel stayed put. Gingerly sitting up, he flexed his jaw, then slowly wiped away the blood welling from his bottom lip with the back of his hand. He looked consideringly at Taggart, comprehension lighting his jewel-toned eyes. "It's like that, huh?" he said quietly, his expression a mixture of sympathy and dawning regret.

"Yeah. Maybe. Hell—" Taggart raked a hand through his hair impatiently "—I don't know. But yeah," he said finally. "I think so."

The realization struck him like a well-aimed boot to the head. For a second he felt dizzy and weak in the knees, and it didn't get any better as the magnitude of what he might have lost began to dawn on him.

He'd never said a word to her about what he *did* feel, hadn't put himself out enough even to tell her that he cared. And now, unintentionally or not, he'd broken his promise that she wouldn't have to face jail alone. Hell, for all he knew, she might very well think he'd driven off and callously arranged for Gabe to come so he wouldn't have to face her and own up to what she was sure to see as a betrayal.

"Damn, Taggart, I'm sorry."

His brother's voice was a welcome interruption in his tempestuous thoughts. Telling himself that it was more important than ever to focus on the here and now, to concentrate on doing what he could to make this better for Genevieve and deal with his own fear and fury and worry later, he took a deep breath and turned his attention back to Gabe. "What did you say?"

"That I'm sorry. If I'd had a clue—" he stopped, uttered a single, profane word that left no doubt as to the depth of his regret "—it never would've happened."

Taggart knew damn well Gabe was sincere; it wasn't in his brother's nature to be anything but straight with him. Even so, he was in no mood to let him off the hook just yet.

"You *should* be sorry." Reaching down, he offered his hand to the man who'd been the only true constant in his life before Genevieve and yanked him to his feet. "What the hell are you doing here, anyway?"

Gabriel gave an offhand shrug. "It's been nearly a week. After a while, when you didn't check in, Lilah started to get worried—"

"Lilah?" At the mention of their brother Dominic's bride, his eyebrows climbed and his hard-won calm deserted him. "When the hell did *Lilah* get the green light to call the shots and interfere in my life?"

Gabe sighed. "Since Dom found out she's pregnant. Trust me, the next six months are going to be long for all of us."

"Is she all right?" he asked sharply.

"She's fine. Dom's the one who's a wild-eyed maniac."

"Yeah, well I'll deal with him later. Right now, I want to hear what went down with Genevieve."

"You're not going to like it."

"Yeah. I figured." That sick feeling twisted through his gut again and he shook it off. "But for now I'm going to give you a pass." Walking toward the door, he picked up Genevieve's duffel bag and heaved it at Gabe before leaning down and grabbing a box in either arm.

"And why, exactly, is that?" the other man inquired, following him out to the back of the SUV.

"Because." He gave the loose tire a savage shove, stowed the books and turned to face his brother. "You're about to help me do whatever it takes to get Genevieve out of jail."

Again, Gabriel searched his face, then gave the faintest of sighs. "I suppose that means we're going to have to clear the brother?"

"Didn't I just say whatever it takes?" he countered, pushing past Gabe to head back to the cabin for the rest of their stuff.

Yet as he stepped inside, he felt that old, familiar bleakness settle over his heart. Because while exonerating Seth Bowen might be enough to secure Genevieve's freedom, he wasn't at all sure it would be enough to make her give him another chance.

That is, if he deserved one at all.

Fourteen

Clutching her coat, Genevieve stepped out onto the wide front steps of the Silver County Jail. After nine days spent inside, locked up in a ten-by-ten cell that had sported a single narrow, mesh-covered window, the afternoon sunlight was as welcome as it was dazzling.

She drank in several long draughts of pristine air, took a moment to enjoy the briskness of the day, then squeezed her eyes shut and said a silent prayer of thanks for her freedom.

Despite the assurances of her attorney, who had informed her he'd been engaged on her behalf by Steele Security, Genevieve still found it hard to believe that the nightmare that had consumed more than eight months of her life was finally over.

Yet the reality was driven home as she heard footsteps coming up the stairs and opened her eyes to find a familiar male face smiling crookedly down at her.

"Seth!" For one incredulous moment she could only stare at her baby brother. And then joy picked her up and sent her flying into his arms. "Oh, God, you're out! You're really free!"

Laughing and crying at once, she clung to him, patting, stroking, touching—his hands, his arms, his precious, precious face—needing that solid contact to assure herself he was really there, really all right. "I can't believe it. When? How?"

"This morning," he said, burying his face in her hair and holding on to her with the same kind of fierceness he'd displayed when he'd needed comfort as a little boy. "It was Laura's brother, Gen. He was the one. He killed Jimmy."

Her hands went still. "What?" she said in disbelief, leaning back to stare in shock at his face. "It was Martin? But why?"

"Turns out that's not his name. And he really isn't Laura's brother at all, but her lover," Seth said, more than a trace of hardness glinting in his eyes. With a little jolt, Genevieve realized that in the months since she'd seen him the last trace of boyish softness had left his face and that he was finally, fully, a man.

"They planned it from the start," he went on. "Apparently they were looking for somebody like Jimmy even before they met him. Then later, I guess Jimmy told Laura what he told me—that he'd changed beneficiaries—so they went ahead. It was supposed to look like he'd walked in on a burglary, just like I thought, only I showed up and drove Martin off before he could stage it."

"But…" Genevieve tried to take it in, to wrap her mind around it. "He was with Jimmy's folks…wasn't he?"

"Laura was. Turns out Martin was a little late, claimed he'd gotten lost finding the house. Which nobody thought to mention, since I got tagged right away."

"But the will, the insurance—"

"You know Jimmy. He was always putting things off, talking about stuff like it was a done deal before he even got the ball rolling." He shook his head. "Damn, but I miss him."

The reminder of everything he'd been through had her winding her arms around his middle and giving him another fervent hug. "I know. I know. I'm just so glad the rest of this is over."

"Yeah. Me, too." He allowed himself one more moment of comfort, then got a grip on himself. Straightening, he gently set her away, smoothed her hair back behind her ears.

There was a space of silence while they both simply stood and smiled at each other. "So?" he said finally, lifting an eyebrow. "You going to ask me who's responsible for us standing here like this or not?"

"I'm pretty sure I already know," she said, swallowing hard and telling herself she was not going to let anything spoil this moment.

That Seth was here, free, meant she owed John a debt she could never repay. The fact that she hadn't seen or heard from him since she'd been hauled away from the cabin didn't matter.

Or it shouldn't. No. It didn't. She refused to let it. She'd known there were no guarantees right from the start, known even as she was falling in love with him that their time in Montana might be all they ever had.

Just as she knew, with a certainty that didn't require reassurance or proof, that he'd had nothing to do with that last, terrifying scene at the cabin. Whatever had gone wrong, it hadn't been his fault.

"I like him," Seth volunteered.

"You've met?"

"Sure. We've talked a bunch of times, while I was in jail, then again earlier today, after I got out."

"He's a good person, a good man," she said firmly.

"Yeah. Except—" he made a soft sound that was a uniquely male mix of amusement and sympathy with just a hint of good-natured derision "—I think he's scared."

"John?" She didn't believe it for a minute. After what he'd been through in Afghanistan, she doubted anything could faze him. But she also knew her brother well enough to see he was dying for her to ask the question anyway and she was too glad to see him to deny him anything. "Of what?"

He paused just a moment, clearly enjoying himself. "You."

"Me?" she exclaimed. "That's ridiculous."

"Hey, don't kill the messenger." He raised his hands in surrender. "It's just my opinion. The guy didn't say five words on the drive over, but I could tell it was killing him to hang back at the car. One of his brothers, Dominic, I think, claims he's walking proof that the bigger they are, the harder they fall."

"John's here?"

"Yeah. Didn't I just say that?"

But Genevieve wasn't listening.

Stepping around Seth, she lifted her hand to shield her eyes from the sun as she surveyed the busy street. It only took a second for her gaze to fix on the tall man with the warrior's face staring back at her as he stood stiffly beside the shiny black SUV parked at the far curb.

Her coat fell forgotten to the ground as her heart trumped her common sense and sent her leaping down the remaining steps. She checked her motion for an instant on the sidewalk, took a quick look at the traffic and then dashed into the street.

Ignoring the bark of a horn and the screech of brakes, she dodged around a pair of cars and flung herself into his arms.

"Oh, God, I wasn't going to do this," she said, burying her face in his neck as she nearly knocked him off his feet. "And you don't have to say anything, I understand you don't feel the way I do, and I don't expect anything, really, but I've just missed you. I've missed you so much."

"Genevieve." Taggart could barely get her name out past the lump jamming his throat. He'd thought he was prepared for anything. Anger. Disdain. Demands to know where the hell he'd been. Even a sincere but distant declaration of thanks before she brushed him off and walked out of his life.

The only thing he hadn't expected was this. That she'd come straight at him with her arms wide open, her heart on her sleeve, and wrap him in the priceless gift of her love, no questions, no demands for an explanation, no words of reproach.

Squeezing his eyes shut, he locked his arms around her and lifted her effortlessly up, some of the terrible tension that had made it hard for him to get a deep breath the past ten days finally easing. Not one to hang back, she promptly wrapped her legs around his waist and twined her arms around his neck and held on like she'd never let him go.

His heart. His miracle. His love.

The woman who'd gotten the drop on him, whisked away the cloud of darkness surrounding him and taught him how to laugh again.

Until this moment he'd told himself that if it was what she wanted, he'd let her go. Yet with her safely in his arms, he could finally admit to himself that that was a lie.

She was his now. Just like he was hers.

And the least that he owed her was to tell the truth, do his best to explain why, when she'd needed him most, he hadn't been there for her.

"Genevieve," he said again, his voice stronger this time.

"Hmm?"

"You need to look at me. You have a right—" he stopped and swallowed, a hard man reduced to jelly by a woman with a Pollyanna complex "—to see my face when I tell you this."

Loosening the stranglehold she had on him, she leaned back. "Whatever it is—"

"Shh," he ordered. He'd meant to work his way up to this, but when he saw the worry suddenly darkening her eyes, he knew that he had to just say it, straight out. "Just listen. When I came back and found out what

Gabe had done—I was more afraid than I've ever been. Somehow, you'd made me take another look at what happened that night on Zari Pass, made me at least consider that I might not be the only one responsible, made me start to think that maybe, maybe, I could have a...real life. With you.

"But it was all so new, the last thing I ever expected. And then, when it was too late, when I came back and found you were gone, I just got all tangled up inside. Rather than come and see you and take the chance that you'd tell me to get the hell out and leave you alone, I thought—if I could just make things right for you and Seth—maybe then you'd believe that I hadn't just gone off and double-crossed you.

"And then, the longer it took, when the judge proved difficult and the whole thing dragged on and I was still a no-show... Well, you've got every reason to tell me to go, except—"

"It's all right," Genevieve interrupted, unwilling to allow him another second of self-doubt, wanting him to know she'd believed in him all along.

"No, it's not. Damn it, Genevieve, what I'm trying to say is—" his voice hitched just for an instant, then turned steady and strong "—I love you. I love you and I want us to be together. Forever. Say you'll be my wife."

"Oh, John." Genevieve's heart hitched as she stared into the warm green flame of his eyes. There were no longer any shadows lurking there, she realized, just a steady, blazing light. "I love you, too. Always."

"Is that a yes?"

She smiled. "How could I possibly turn down such a romantic proposal? Absolutely it's a yes."

To her amazement, he closed his eyes, obviously overcome, just for a second.

And then he was looking straight at her, his mouth slowly curving up in a smile with nothing held back.

To her shock, she saw that there was a tantalizing crease bracketing one side of his mouth that looked suspiciously like a dimple.

Then she forgot everything else as he said, "Thank God. That'll save me the job of having to chase you down again and chain *you* to a bed." Dipping his head, he kissed her, hot and sweet and tender.

And Genevieve kissed him back, knowing it was a preview and a promise of their future.

Epilogue

Genevieve sipped a glass of champagne as she stood in Gabriel Steele's handsomely furnished living room.

As much as she was enjoying her wedding reception, it was nice to have a moment to just catch her breath, reflect a little, take a look around.

People—a lot of whom were tall, striking, dark-haired men—were either scattered around the room or standing out on the terrace that wrapped the lighted swimming pool. Two of the latter happened to be John and Seth, who were listening intently to something being said by a third man she thought was either Deke or Cooper. Or was that Jake?

Candles scented the air with masculine fragrances of spice and sandalwood. Music played, a soft backdrop for the steady hum of conversation punctuated by occasional bursts of laughter.

At the other end of the room, her best friend Kate caught her eye, made a show of panning the room and its phalanx of good-looking, eligible men, mimed the word *wow* and then fanned herself, making Genevieve smile.

It was hard to believe she'd been a married woman for eight entire hours now.

Just before noon that day, she and John, accompanied by Seth, Kate, Dominic's stunning wife Lilah, and all of the Steele brothers except for the three deployed overseas, had walked out to the small, perfect meadow nestled like a jewel on the edge of the wilderness that stretched behind her house.

There, beside the little pond sparkling like glass under the pale fall sun, in the place where she'd made a home for herself, wearing the loveliest cream and ivory antique lace dress she'd ever seen, surrounded by the people she loved most and a profusion of extravagantly colored chrysanthemums, she and John had stood before a minister and exchanged their vows.

It had been beyond perfect, she reflected, glancing down at the simple emerald and diamond band that now graced her left hand.

Just the blindingly beautiful fall day, with the wind whispering through the grass and the sun kissing her cheeks. And John. Tall and straight and solemn, pledging her his love for the rest of their lives.

It had been everything she'd ever hoped for. Far more than she'd ever expected to have. And it was only the beginning.

"Genevieve? Can I get you anything? Some more champagne?"

She glanced up to find Gabriel standing before her. Handsome and charismatic, with beautiful manners—as long as he didn't think you might have harmed someone he loved—John's elegant, slightly enigmatic brother continued to knock himself out trying to make up for his rough treatment of her.

He'd not only been instrumental in securing her freedom, enlisting the governor as well as one of the state's senators to go to bat for her, but she'd had only to mention to him how she envisioned her wedding and he'd promptly taken care of all of the details, then insisted on throwing them this party.

"I'm fine, Gabriel," she said with a smile. "Or I will be, once you agree to forget about what happened between us at the cabin." She touched her hand to his sleeve. "Believe me, I know what it feels like to do whatever seems necessary to safeguard a brother you love."

"Yes." He considered her, and something in his face seemed to lighten even before he smiled. "I suppose you do." Then to her astonishment, he leaned over and kissed her gently on the cheek. "John's lucky to have you," he murmured, before he straightened, smiled again and strolled away.

Bemused, she was trying to decide what she thought she'd heard in his voice—a touch of wistfulness, a hint of loneliness?—when a pair of strong arms settled around her waist.

Everything else ceased to matter as she felt John's solid warmth at her back. "You okay?" he said softly, pressing a kiss to the sensitive patch of skin behind her ear.

"Perfect, now that you're here." Turning in the circle of his arms, she looked at him.

In sharp contrast to Gabe, who'd been the picture of sartorial splendor, John had already shed his tie and jacket. The neck of his pristine white shirt was open, exposing his strong, bronzed throat, while his sleeves were rolled to just below his elbows.

He looked big and tough and so gorgeously male that she couldn't contain a sigh of pure pleasure. "How about you?" She reached up, ostensibly to smooth his hair while actually just wanting to touch him.

"I'm doing all right. He caught her hand, cradled it against the curve of his face. "But I'd be even better if I could talk you into getting out of here with me." He slid her palm to his mouth and pressed a kiss to it that made her flush.

"I'm tired of sharing," he said softly. "I want you all to myself."

"Then I'm your girl. You may not have heard—" she leaned in, went up on tiptoe and nibbled at his bottom lip "—but I'm extremely good at disappearing."

John felt his lips quirk up as he angled his head and claimed her mouth for a brief but heated kiss. With Genevieve, life was always going to be interesting, filled with light no matter what the weather.

Tracking her down had been the best thing ever to happen to him. And if it took him the rest of his life, he meant to make sure she felt the same way.

Starting right now, he vowed, as they both straightened, joined hands and made their escape.

* * * * *

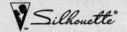

THE
ELLIOTTS

Mixing business with pleasure

The series continues with

Cause for Scandal

by
ANNA DePALO

(Silhouette Desire #1711)

She posed as her identical twin to meet a sexy rock star—but Summer Elliott certainly didn't expect to end up in bed with him. Now the scandal is about to hit the news and she has some explaining to do...to her prominent family and her lover.

On sale March 2006!

e✦HARLEQUIN.com

The Ultimate Destination for Women's Fiction

Calling all aspiring writers!
Learn to craft the perfect romance novel with our useful tips and tools:

- Take advantage of our **Romance Novel Critique Service** for detailed advice from romance professionals.

- Use our **message boards** to connect with writers, published authors and editors.

- Enter our **Writing Round Robin—** you could be published online!

- Learn many tools of the writer's trade from editors and authors in our **On Writing** section!

- **Writing guidelines** for Harlequin or Silhouette novels—what our editors *really* look for.

Learn more about romance writing from the experts—
visit www.eHarlequin.com today!

Silhouette

Desire

WHAT HAPPENS IN VEGAS...

Shock! Proud casino owner
Hayden MacKenzie's former fiancée,
who had left him at the altar for a cool
one million dollars, was back in Sin City.
It was time for the lovely Shelby Paxton
to pay in full—starting with the wedding
night they never had....

His Wedding-Night Wager

by **Katherine Garbera**

On sale February 2006 (SD #1708)

Also look for:

Her High-Stakes Affair, March 2006
Their Million-Dollar Night, April 2006

From reader-favorite
Kathie DeNosky

THE ILLEGITIMATE HEIRS

A brand-new miniseries about three brothers denied a father's name, but granted a special inheritance.

Don't miss:

Engagement between Enemies

(Silhouette Desire #1700,
on sale January 2006)

Reunion of Revenge

(Silhouette Desire #1707,
on sale February 2006)

Betrothed for the Baby

(Silhouette Desire #1712,
on sale March 2006)

COMING NEXT MONTH

SDCNM0206